SAVAGE HEAT

Mandy Monroe

Paranormal Romance

New Concepts

Georgia

Be sure to check out our website for the very best in fiction at fantastic prices!

When you visit our webpage, you can:
* Read excerpts of currently available books
* View cover art of upcoming books and current releases
* Find out more about the talented artists who capture the magic of the writer's imagination on the covers
* Order books from our backlist
* Find out the latest NCP and author news--including any upcoming book signings by your favorite NCP author
* Read author bios and reviews of our books
* Get NCP submission guidelines
* And so much more!

Be sure to visit our webpage to find the best deals in e-books and paperbacks! To find out about our new releases as soon as they are available, please be sure to sign up for our newsletter (http://www.newconceptspublishing.com/newsletter.htm) or join our reader group (http://groups.yahoo.com/group/new_concepts_pub/join)!

The newsletter is available by double opt in only and our customer information is *never* shared!

Visit our webpage at:
www.newconceptspublishing.com

Savage Heat is an original publication of NCP. This work has never before appeared in book form. This work is a novel. Any similarity to actual persons or events is purely coincidental.

New Concepts Publishing, Inc.
5202 Humphreys Rd.
Lake Park, GA 31636

NCP books are available at special quantity discounts for bulk purchases for sales promotions, premiums, fund raising, or educational use. For details, write, email, or phone New Concepts Publishing, Inc., 5202 Humphreys Rd., Lake Park, GA 31636; Ph. 229-257-0367, Fax 229-219-1097; orders@newconceptspublishing.com.

First NCP Trade Paperback Printing: September 2010

Chapter One

With a whoop of glee, Emma danced on the spot for a second or two of unbridled pleasure. Not even an orgasm could feel this damned good. Eyes gleaming in triumph, she pumped her fist into the air. It was at times like these she wished that she had someone to share her almost-successes with but, with a shrug of her shoulders, she relinquished that thought and continued to dance where she stood, celebrating the taste of success her latest findings suggested.

Rechecking the read-out her printer had just spat out, she rejoiced in the fact that her pheromone was finally ready for a trial run! The last specimen she'd concocted had been so close to what she needed! It was damned great to know that this one was the most promising specimen yet. Maybe it was a bad idea to let herself get caught up in the idea that this was one would do the trick. Being a scientist, she knew she should wait for concrete facts, but she couldn't help but feel it in her gut. Number ten was the culmination of over four years of hard work and countless years of study.

It couldn't come at a better time, either. Her grant was ready for renewal and she had to have definite proof that the money the university was spending on her and her experiments was actually worth something!

A tinge of doubt tainted her happy smile. This pheromone was so important, not just for her or her profession or even her future, but for the creatures she'd come to care for over the course of her career. These studies had become her life and if this pheromone worked in the way she believed it would, it meant that she'd accomplished her goal.

Just thinking she was close to success, that all these

years had actually been worthwhile, made her feel a little dizzy. Sitting down with an unceremonious plop on her lab stool, she closed her eyes and prayed that the figures and readings were right, prayed that number ten was her lucky number. Her work was so important, so vital to the wolf population in America, whose numbers were dwindling more rapidly every year. This pheromone could change all of that. If the figures were right, and the pheromone sailed through the trials, it would be ready for mass-production on not just a national level but an international scale.

Tamping her euphoria, Emma tried not to get ahead of herself. The future looked good. She wouldn't deny that, but she couldn't be too sure of herself. The test trials would tell her everything she needed to know. It was as simple and as frightening as that. Everything she'd worked so hard for now hung in the balance and the control freak in her screamed at the need to wait, to calculate, to test, to observe, to document.

She knew what her problem was. She'd lost all objectivity a long time ago, a huge danger for any scientist, but especially her. The pheromone had become her obsession. She *had* to find a way to increase the wolf population. It had become her lifeblood, her food, her water. Not a day had passed during the last four years where she hadn't worked on some aspect of the production of this chemical. It had taken over her life but she couldn't, wouldn't, ever regret a single moment of it. To her, wolves were . . . . As pathetic as it sounded, they'd become her friends a long time ago. A loner since birth, she'd soon softened towards the wild animals under her observation and that had blossomed with time as they had accepted her.

As weird and unlikely and impossible as it sounded, they really had, the wild beasts had allowed her to poke and prod when she knew damn well that they rarely allowed close contact. They allowed her to go near them, the new mothers had allowed her to touch their pups, to check their health. They had trusted her not to harm them and she hadn't. She'd become attached to them and now they were the main focus of her existence. This pheromone was their future, she knew that and that was why it consumed her life.

Wolves were wonderful creatures, individually and as a pack, their behavior and interaction were delightfully simple to analyze, there was no way for them to lie or cheat. Their mentality was to survive and all that entailed. A part of her wished humans interacted in the same simple manner. As a loner, she had sat on the fringe of friendships and played witness to the true lows of human behavior and preferred not to be around them. Their complex natures lent themselves easily to deception, and, in truth, she preferred not to be a part of it. Now her respect for the wolves was such that it was imperative she give aid to the creatures who had become her friends a long time ago.

Stretching slightly, she got to her feet, more steady now, and headed towards the small fridge that housed the tenth version of the pheromone. Her mouth quirked into a small grin as she mentally crossed her fingers, toes, and unmentionables, while she transferred the precious chemical from its glass container into a plastic bottle via a pipette. Releasing the liquid with a gush, she screwed the spray nozzle on to the cap then carefully stuck it in her pocket.

Spinning on her toes, Emma walked through her small, sterile laboratory and into her favorite room in the cabin, the family room. Not that she had a family to share it with, but apart from her lab, it was where she spent the majority of her time and had decorated it thusly. It was an immensely comfortable room, yet practical and elegant at the same time. Not that she ever had guests which was nice because she'd been able to make the room just the way she wanted to without having to worry about what anyone else would think.

The carpet was a lush deep green color and reminded her of a lawn. She had known upon purchasing it that it would give the room an entirely natural ambiance. It was a perfect square-shaped room. Two of the walls had large picture windows that allowed her to look out at the woods that surrounded her house. The huge panes of glass opened up the room to the wild elements and enabled her to just sit and watch the swaying trees on quiet evenings. On some nights she could play silent witness to the ravages of a storm, watch the rain lash against the wood like a leather whip, see the wind sweep the loam angrily away. It was more entertaining than any TV show.

Directly in the center of the third wall was a small fireplace that she lit in winter to ward off the chill. To the left of the fireplace sat a TV stand. Constructed entirely out of driftwood, it looked so unsteady as to be absurd. She often looked at it and wondered how the TV actually stayed on it, but it did and the little used machine sat there, more often than not, silently. Just to the right of the fireplace and a little in front of it sat her pride and joy, a huge armchair that was basically a huge square upon which she could sit dead center with miles of space around her. She could lay flat on it comfortably it was so large. She'd spent many a night asleep on that chair, the fire flickering gently in front of her, her papers resting on her knee during her slumber. Beside the armchair stood a standard lamp also constructed from driftwood, long strips of the stuff were clustered together and upon them rested a large cream oval lampshade, which when illuminated gave off a soft, golden glow.

She'd designed the space to be as natural and simple as possible, and even now, just passing through it, the room acted as a calming, soothing salve to her jittery excited nerves. All the rooms were basic. She wasn't one for intense bright colors nor did she feel a need for things cluttered around her. She enjoyed simplicity. It enabled her to concentrate and relax. Her bedroom was similarly designed for comfort, a large king size bed sat in the center of the room beside which stood two more standard lamps and that was it. She liked minimalism.

With a smile, she headed into her kitchen, leaned

over the sink, which also had a window that allowed her to look out at the woods, and picked up the small remote that lay on the windowsill behind her work top and stuck that in her other pocket.

At one time, the house had belonged to a grounds keeper, the land owned by a multi-national conglomerate with a green conscience. They had eventually donated the land to the government for preservation and the house had been left vacant, left on a Realtors books for rent, but as it was so deeply hidden, it had remained empty. It may have been on the edge of the woods and not exactly in them, but it was still damned hard to find—another reason she loved it! This year was her fourth year and she would continue to live here even if this trial proved successful. The solitude might have been horrific for a lot of people, but she reveled in it, had in fact never been so productive. She had managed to accomplish so much here and knew it was because of the solitude. Never being disturbed meant that she could concentrate, and, when she focused, it was surprising how much she could get done. She knew for certain that had she been elsewhere, her work on the pheromone would have necessitated eight years rather than the four it had.

For many reasons, her home appealed to her, she loved the land it rested upon, adored that the forest was her only neighbor. Her search for a suitable research area four years ago had led her here, for there was a considerable wolf population within the grounds, and then on looking around, the beauty had worked its magic on her, as well. It had charmed her so utterly, so completely, that it had been imperative she live here, no matter the cost. That it was perfect as her home and for work, was just the cherry on top of an already gorgeous cake!

With a slight whistle, she headed into her small garage through the connecting door and stopped mid tune as her lips twitched at the reproachful gaze that followed her journey towards the cage that lay in the very center of the room.

She smiled softly at the she-wolf in the large cage, checking to make sure her food and water dispenser were full before she bent into a crouch beside the beautiful animal and whispered, "I'm so sorry, honey. But you'll see, it's been worth it, I promise." She grinned as the wolf didn't budge an inch, just sat silently in the roomy cage and watched her with baleful eyes. It was rather a shocking scene because the wolf was so totally at ease with her and she was so comfortable with the wolf. To anyone looking in, it would have been rather surreal because the creature didn't snarl or snap, wasn't at all aggressive. The wolf was obviously just waiting for the woman to release her. There was a bizarre trust at play here, and Emma was fully aware of that. It was one of the reasons she'd dedicated her life to creating this pheromone. Wolves were the only thing on this Earth that accepted her. She couldn't very well then afford to lose them.

It was as simple and crazy as that.

"You'll soon be free, sweetie, and hopefully pregnant!" Emma crooned softly at the animal. She knew that they didn't understand her, but being alone all the time had made her treat them as other human beings. If people could talk to plants in the hope that they'd grow because they were loved then she would do exactly the same thing with the she-wolves she had to trap for her test trials!

Standing up, she brushed the dirt from her knees, walked over to the garage door and, twisting the knob, grimaced as the door opened with a creaky groan. Making a mental note to oil it, she returned to the cage, and, curling her fingers around one of the handles attached to the large box, she began her arduous trek to the nearby cluster of trees where she'd noticed the wolves gathered. It wasn't far by any means, but it was difficult on foot and even more difficult with a cage to lug. She had no other choice but to walk, though. The sound of a vehicle would create too much fuss in the woodland, something she couldn't afford to happen.

Even a trailer would cause too much noise. The sound of her dragging it along on the skids would disturb the creatures, but she'd discovered in the past that it didn't frighten them overly.

Pulling the cage from her garage, she found herself almost immediately in the woods. Her cabin was on the very edge of the woods and was perfect for her studies. She was thankful she didn't have far to walk, the cage was very heavy and because of the size and the wolf inside of it, extremely cumbersome. It was originally fitted with heavy-duty wheels on the bottom, but that didn't make it any easier to move the thing. In fact, as soon as she got it on soft ground it bogged down and was harder to move than if it had had no wheels at all. It didn't take long to discover that wasn't going to work! Trapping the she-wolves was a necessary part of the work. She hated doing it, but there was no other way to test the pheromone, and, upon realizing there was no other way to test the chemical in their natural surroundings, she'd determined to design a cage herself, one that fit her exact specifications and that at least provided a modicum of comfort for the creatures. It had cost a fortune, had in fact taken up a huge chunk of her first small grant, but it had been worth it—Well, once she'd gotten the moving figured out and swapped the wheels for skids that at least made it possible to pull the cage over the grounds and into the woods.

There had been other options open to her. She could have tested the pheromone on the more domestic creatures in zoos and wildlife sanctuaries, but she had known that the pheromone needed to be tested in the wolves' natural surroundings. That decision had caused her a lot of grief, but it had been worth it.

Panting as she dragged the cage, she grumbled when she tripped over a rock. Immediately releasing the handle to steady herself, she bent over, propping her hands on her knees while she caught her breath. Deeply inhaling the lushly fragrant air, she released a small sigh of satisfaction. That scent could make her heart beat like nothing else could. She loved the woods, loved them with a passion. The silence, compared to the bustle of the city, was deafening at times and could be very repressive to some people, she knew, but it soothed her soul. Deciding to live on the edge of the wood had been the best decision she had ever made. There was a freedom here that could be found nowhere else. Living so far from everyone else meant that, at any time, day or night, she could go for a walk. There were no interfering neighbors, no one to watch her or think her odd because she herself kept odd hours. She often wandered through the woods at night, the leafy atmosphere relaxing her every time, and on returning home, she would immediately fall into the deepest of slumbers. In her twenty-nine years on this Earth, she could safely say that she had never slept so well as she had since she'd moved out here.

Rested, she focused on her task once more, keeping watch all the time for the landmarks that led her to the area the wolves tended to frequent. When at last she spied the tree trunk with a great big hole in the center, pleasure chased her weariness. For once she'd managed the task without incident. Of course, she had tripped, but she'd managed to right herself and hadn't fallen to the ground.

Usually, she ended up spraining or at least straining something. She'd never been known for her graceful coordination, she thought wryly. In fact she'd always tended to be a little clumsy. She liked to think she'd grown out of it, and that it was mostly enthusiasm and no caution rather than a lack of coordination anyway, but there was no getting around the fact that she usually managed to bruise and bang herself up on her treks into the woods even when she succeeded in avoiding straining a muscle. Tomorrow her arms and back would probably protest the heavy lifting, but this time, thankfully, that was it.

Almost there! The adrenaline rush from starting a new test added to her jitters, her already weak arms trembling slightly at the exertion. Huffing and puffing now, she stopped to rest for a second. She bent over once more to lean her hands against her thighs and managed to slow her breathing.

Although her movements had been relatively quiet in comparison to the difficulty of the task, she knew that any wildlife would have fled at even the softest of sounds. This was perfect for her experiment, though. If the pheromone worked, the scent would bring the wolves she'd scared off running back in spite of the noise or whatever scent she'd left. It would have them eagerly congregating around the cage.

Still bent over and struggling for breath, Emma reached for the bottle in her pocket, wrinkling her nose when she grabbed the bottle by the top instead of the side and squirted some of the precious pheromone in her palm. Grimacing, she snatched her hand back and wiped it on the seat of her pants. Discovering she still had it between her fingers, she tugged her strappy t-shirt out of her jeans and used the hem to dry between her fingers. Grumbling now with irritation, she retrieved the bottle from her pocket and moved around the cage to douse the she-wolf in the chemical. The creature responded with a little growl as the spray touched her snout, but other than that she seemed undisturbed.

When she was satisfied she'd thoroughly doused the wolf in pheromones, Emma crossed her fingers tightly and jogged to her landmark tree. The hole in the center of the trunk allowed her to peer into the small clearing, but she was hidden by the thick tree so she could observe without disturbing the wolves.

Excitement churned through her, making her breathless with anticipation now where she'd been breathless with exertion before. In the blink of an eye, she'd completely forgotten about her aches and pains, her focus switching to the she-wolf and the admirers she hoped would soon come running.

Cautioning herself that she might have a long wait even if she was right and the pheromones did work, Emma tried to slow her excited breathing. She needed to get a grip, she told herself. It was all very well to be excited and filled with enthusiasm, but she needed to keep an open mind and make scientific observations. If the wolves appeared and began milling around the cage that would *probably* mean that the pheromone she'd developed worked, but the only way to be positive it was that and nothing else would be to try it many times and see if she got the same results. Nobody was going to accept one incident as proof. She'd have to be able to *repeat* the experiment and get the same results to prove her pheromone worked.

Of course, the female wasn't in heat and, to her mind that meant, if she drew the males, it was damned conclusive, but she couldn't afford to get ahead of herself if she wanted to be taken seriously!

The 'ifs' tumbling around in her mind made her feel like screaming with impatience, but she closed her eyes and focused on achieving an acceptable level of calm. The sound of a twig crunching close by made her eyes snap wide open. Hoping it wasn't merely a branch creaking in the wind, she held her breath, searching until her gaze finally settled on the source— a wolf! Delight wafted through her, intensifying when she spotted several more.

Hesitantly at first, clearly wary—probably because they caught her scent and suspected a trap!—the male wolves lifted their heads and sniffed the air. After a few moments, they left the cover of the brush and approached the caged she-wolf. Treading delicately towards her, pausing every few steps to scan the clearing and the woods, they inched closer, obviously as suspicious of the scent that had attracted them to her as they were of the scent of Emma near the cage, but unable to help themselves. Upon reaching it at last, they began to sniff the entirety of the rectangular box, pressing their snouts eagerly against the meshed walls, investigating the bored looking she-wolf.

A rush of joy went through Emma as she watched them. Her pheromone actually worked! It worked! She struggled with the urge to perform a victory dance as she had earlier when she'd just *thought* she had the formula! The pleasure she'd experienced earlier paled in comparison to this intense feeling of happiness, though. If that was an orgasm, she thought with a mixture of supreme satisfaction and amusement, abruptly grinning broadly, *this* must be what a multiple orgasm felt like!

She didn't realize she actually *was* bobbing and wiggling her ass in a little dance of glee until she abruptly felt something poke her in the ass—actually wedged between the cheeks of her ass. It took all she could do to keep from jumping straight up and giving herself away, but she couldn't refrain from whipping a look behind her.

There was a wolf directly behind her with his snout burrowed between the cheeks of her ass!

It was clear from the way his eyeballs were rolled back into his head that he liked the smell—which was when it abruptly dawned on Emma that she'd wiped the damned pheromone on the seat of her jeans when she'd accidentally gotten it on her hand!

Horror instantly replaced her glee of moments before. Panic washed over her when she discovered two others had jolted to a halt when she'd whipped around.

She'd drawn as many males as the she-wolf in the damned cage!

She was too panicked to think what the hell to do once she recalled that she'd coated herself with the damned pheromone—which obviously worked a lot better than she'd realized! She couldn't possibly have gotten that much on *her*, she thought angrily! She'd sprayed the she-wolf down thoroughly. They ought to be at the damned cage with the others! They ought not to be able to smell it on her over the she-wolf!

Unless she'd caught some of the mist, as well, she thought in sudden horror?

No! She couldn't think like that and she hadn't noticed, she reassured herself. She'd just gotten it on her hand and wiped it on her clothes.

That realization finally prompted a possibility for

escape. The moment it occurred to her, uneasiness wafted through her. The idea of stripping down for a bunch of horny wolves seemed like a very poor one, but the pheromones had clearly raised their aggression. Running was never a good idea, and it was an especially poor one under the circumstances.

There was no hope for it! They'd back off a little once they'd discovered the scent that had drawn them masked the fact that it was a human female, and not a she wolf, but they didn't seem inclined to dismiss her and join the wolves at the damned cage. In point of fact, it looked to her like they were working themselves up to duke it out over which of them was going to get to mount her first!

She was shaking like a leaf when she began trying to wiggle out of her clothes without making any sudden moves that might antagonize them.

The bizarre sense flickered through her mind when she eased her t-shirt up her belly and discovered she had the undivided attention of the wolves that she was doing a strip tease for a pack of wolves and for a moment she struggled with the slightly hysterical urge to giggle.

The look in the wolves eyes killed it. In fact, it scared the hell out of her when she discovered she'd actually met the lead wolf's gaze! She knew better that that! It was like issuing a challenge!

He growled low in his throat, and she quickly trained her gaze on the ground. The really unnerving moment came when she had to pull the t-shirt off over her head and was momentarily blinded. To her relief, instead of rushing her, she discovered the wolves had sat down to watch, their heads tilted curiously.

Instead of dropping the t-shirt once she'd removed it, she held it in one shaking hand while she unfastened her jeans and began to wiggle out of them. The bottle was still in the pocket and she hated like hell to abandon it, but she had the formula, she reminded herself! She could reproduce it if she didn't get eaten!

She had to push her shoes off to get the damned jeans

all the way off. Easing them off, she stepped out of the jeans and then dropped the t-shirt next to her jeans and shoved her feet into her shoes again. Very slowly, she began to sidle away from the pile of clothes that obviously wreaked with mating pheromones.

The wolves watched her, but to her relief, that was all they did—beyond growling low in their throats. She paused at the warning, waiting until she'd regained control of her runaway heart, and then began to inch a little further away.

The distance between her and the house, which had never seemed very far at all, seemed to stretch in her mind as she thought in dismay about just how far she was going to have to go to reach safety. Pushing it from her mind, she focused on trying to 'feel' her way without giving the wolves her back. She didn't know what they might do if she sprawled out and she didn't want to find out!

Moments turned to hours and minutes to days as she slowly worked her way toward the house and away from the clearing. She'd just begun to feel some of the sheer terror waning when she decided to see how much distance she'd actually put between her and the wolves and discovered that the wolves were still following her.

Despite every effort to retain her wits, the realization that it hadn't done one bit of good to abandon her clothes sent her into panic mode. Whirling abruptly, she broke into a run, sprinting toward the house as fast as her legs could carry her.

The trail had seemed long when she'd been dragging the heavy cage. Now, staring fearfully at the distance she still had to run, it felt like she had to run a marathon before she would be able to reach the safety of her home. Fighting the urge to close her eyes in fear as she heard the sounds of snarls and growls as they gave chase, she realized in dismay that although her ploy had allowed her to escape the poor position she had been in and gain a little ground, it hadn't stopped them from wanting to chase her. Although she didn't think they actually were, an image almost instantly rose to mind of the wolves at her heels, nipping at the backs of her feet, gathering themselves to pounce on her. From there, it leapt to an image of them pushing her to the ground and swarming over her, biting and ripping her flesh apart until the lifeblood drained from her and soaked the forest floor, making her forever a part of the woods she had grown to love. Shuddering at the thought, her fear threatening to swamp her, she whipped a fearful look back to see how close they were to catching up with her and making those images a reality.

They weren't as close as she'd feared—actually thought they ought to be—but they were gaining on her. She'd just returned her attention to the path in front of her when she hooked her foot in a protruding root. Her momentum slammed her into the ground so hard it punched the breath from her, knocked her witless for several moments. It was only the residual flight instinct that prompted her to try to struggle to get up even as she fought to fill her lungs with air again. She managed to roll to her side and push herself up on one arm. Catching sight of the wolves, she froze, staring at the deadly predators in wide-eyed horror.

To her amazement, they hesitated instead of launching themselves at her the moment they realized she was helpless. Once more she noticed that they approached delicately and with care, seeming almost hesitant to scare her. Well she felt like yelling at them that it didn't work! She scowled at the crazy thought. Why would they chase her if they didn't want to frighten her? Who heard of animals chasing humans then once they neared the prey making sure to tread carefully? It didn't make any sense. Her troublesome thoughts were gone the instant they were one or two steps away from her. Never in all her years of research had any of the male wolves been so close to her. She stared at them with glassy eyes, but her ears reacted first to the ensuing moment of eerie silence. A hush settled over the woods, so powerful that the shaking of the branches, the rustle of the leaves, the scrabble of a small animal through the loamy floor, were as loud as the beep of a car horn. For some reason, even though they'd stopped moving, their bodies still and somehow waiting, she froze in readiness and in reaction to that bizarre silence. A sixth sense told her something crazy was about to happen. She didn't know what was going on or even how she'd known, but as the wolves' bodies began to twist and contort angrily in front of her, her eyes focused on the movements like a spotlight. She wasn't nearly as horrified as she probably should have been by what happened next.

Bones shuddering, muscles stretching, snouts melting, the wolves' bodies cracked and contorted manically, until finally they started to straighten out, limbs growing from nothing, coming out of misshaped sockets, muscled strong flesh smoothed over a once furred and narrow torso. Before her eyes, three men popped out of the shells of three wolf bodies, their forms lithe and firm, bare to her staring gaze.

Quickly clenching her eyes closed against the sight of the three men standing where three wolves originally had, she gulped and rubbed a hand along her forehead. The scientist asked if the pheromone could possibly contain some sort of hallucinogen, but her instincts knew that her eyes hadn't lied. They had shown her something impossible, but they hadn't lied. Realizing that, she opened them but her head reared back in shock as she saw the naked hunger in their eyes. They hadn't tried to conceal it, lust for her flickered like fire in their penetrating gazes. On a gulp she patted a hand to her head, smoothed it over her skull, checking for bumps. Three wolves had just transformed into men and, if she wasn't mistaken, they wanted to fuck her? Did she have a concussion? Had she somehow within the last five minutes turned from a perfectly rational scientist into a total raving lunatic?

It was somehow easier to believe that men could turn into wolves than it was to believe that these three beautiful specimens could be attracted to her.

Scrambling backwards, hands trying to gain purchase on the ground, she jumped as the men yelled in unison and practically dove atop her. Flinching as they landed near her, she groaned slightly upon realizing that she was trapped with three men who were looking at her like they were the Big Bad Wolves and she was little red. Hating the comparison, she gulped and whispered shakily, unsure if these wolf-men, dare she consider the word werewolves, would understand her, "Am I insane? I know Mom told me that all work and no play would make me dull, but she never told me it would make me crazy!"

One wolf-man chuckled deeply, the sound was gravelly, as though he was unused to both laughter and conversation. "No, you're not insane. You're mine." His words were heavily accented as they razed his throat, and, despite herself, despite the words he spoke, a shudder of pleasure rasped over previously unused nerve endings deep inside her body. The fact that her body was coming to life, to awareness, made her cringe. How could she possibly feel anything for these men who terrified her!

She reared back in shock as the dawning attraction surfaced.

For the other two that were with him, however, his words seemed to inflame them even more. An argument suddenly erupted, words spitting out angrily at each other in another language, one she couldn't understand, although it sounded Eastern European in nature. Hisses and growls and snarls of fury dominated her senses as she watched their fighting ensue. Every look blasted at the other had the power to wound. The muscles in their arms and shoulders clenched threateningly. What they were discussing obviously wasn't easing their anger. If anything it was infuriating them impossibly more.

Never had she felt more scared than at this very moment, and the fear caused her to tremble uncontrollably. Words, body language, and eyes all combined to create an argument terrifying to the witness. As the blond one of the trio hissed a word in a tone far worse than any she'd yet to hear, she flinched in fright. Her slight movement garnered their attention, and she couldn't help but cringe as they stared at her with hungry eyes that seemed to devouring her.

"She's mine, Dante!" Caden growled in an old, forgotten Russian dialect that was only used by their packs, "I saw her first, you bastard."

"Fuck you, Caden, we all saw her at the same time. We were together, remember," Shane reminded his friend with a hiss, his shoulders bunching threateningly.

"She's as much mine as she is yours, Caden," Dante concurred, his attention on the woman more than his friends. Seeing her growing fear, he warned, "You're frightening her!"

"She'll have to get used to my temper," Caden answered arrogantly, "She's mine. I won't share my mate."

"Stop being a bastard, Caden. What gives you the right to her? If one of us saw her first, it was only by a second." Although Dante answered more rationally, his voice was still low and angry, just less so than the other two irate men. "Why should we not claim her because one of us saw her a millisecond before the other? If she's *your* mate, then she's mine and Shane's as well. You say she's yours as though we didn't react to her in exactly the same way as you did! Why should you get her and we shouldn't?"

"What do you suggest? A challenge?" Shane asked, shooting a glare at his childhood friend. "What the fuck's wrong with you?" he asked scornfully as Caden growled menacingly, a partial shift making his eyes glow eerily.

"A challenge is fairer than merely guessing who caught sight of her first!" Dante said simply. "And stop growling like that, Caden. Can't you see she's scared?"

Eyes flashing, Caden took a deep breath, his voice

and body still aggressive as he said, "Her home is over there. It must be the shelter she was running towards. If we allow her return to it, we can sort this challenge out now and I can return to my pack tonight, mate in tow."

Sneering angrily, Shane muttered, "What makes you think you're going to win, you fuck-wit? You're not going to be fighting some lame-assed Beta with designs on being Alpha. Maybe you should reconsider. You must have grown stale on practicing your fighting skills on your bastard weak-kneed Betas."

"Shut up, both of you," Dante commanded, ignoring the glares shot in his direction. "Let's release her and allow her to enter the cabin. Everything we're doing right now is scaring her. We know where she lives now. She cannot flee from us, at least not far without us realizing it." They all rolled away from her as one, and he sighed as his mate immediately scrambled to her feet, ran to her house, and slammed the door shut. Her scent was riddled with fear, it tainted the glorious perfume that radiated from her, making his nose curl in distaste. If his ears didn't deceive him, which they rarely did, he heard the click of the lock on the door as well. Not that it would do her much good. Three Alphas who finally found their mate would not allow a simple lock to stand in their way.

All three watched her hasty retreat to her house. Shane sighed loudly. "A challenge isn't going to work. We're all evenly matched. We're Alphas, for fuck sake. And whoever wins will have their work cut out for them. We just frightened the shit out of her," he finished gloomily.

"A challenge may not be the perfect answer to our problems here, but it will make me feel a damned sight better! She's meant to be with one of us. Whoever wins, and I'm sure it will be me," he paused to glare and curl his lip, "will make her happy. It's fate. A mate cannot fear their other half," Caden said matter-of-factly, interlocking his fingers before cracking his knuckles. Her retreat soothed him slightly, calmed his aggression. He didn't have to fight the need to claim her in front of his friends. His reaction to the small woman should have shocked him, but it was their way. He'd seen other men claim their women. It was perfectly normal for this tension and aggression to riddle their way deep into a man's body.

"How should we do this?" Shane asked.

"The most sensible option is to fight one on one. The winner of the first challenge then proceeds to fight the remaining competitor," Dante said.

"How is that fair? There is only three of us. The winner of the first will be fatigued and fighting against a fresh competitor. If there were four of us, then yes, but we can't do it that way. I refuse to miss out on claiming my mate because I was strong enough to win the first challenge then too tired to win the second!" Shane replied angrily.

On a sigh, Dante considered the options open to them. There weren't all that many. He knew of no challenge that would handle this particular situation. Mates were rarely shared between a group of men, and, if that ever happened, which wasn't often, it wouldn't be between three Alphas of the three most powerful packs in the US! There was no correct protocol for this kind of situation and his next statement showed it, "Free for all," Dante suggested on a grunt and the other two nodded in agreement.

"Whatever the result of this challenge, we need to all swear that we'll uphold it! No changing your mind because you don't win, alright?" Caden told them arrogantly.

With a growl, Dante nodded and Shane snarled his agreement. Clambering to his feet, Dante stood in front of his childhood best friends and for the first time in his life sized them up for battle. Recalling any and every injury they had ever had, every weakness he knew of, he analyzed each and every single one and decided on them accordingly. Never in his life would he have imagined challenging Caden and Shane, but for his woman he had to, for the woman that feared him he would kill his brothers-by-oath, for the woman that was the other half of his soul he would do whatever necessary to ensure that she remained by his side, forever. With a loud roar, Dante charged Caden with his shoulder, hitting him directly in the stomach where three months earlier a Beta had ripped his side clean open.

Having latched the door closed, locked all three locks, and placed the hall's console table directly underneath the doorknob, Emma breathed a sigh of relief. She didn't know why, but they had released her, had allowed her to run back to the safety of her home. They either had felt sorry for her, which she doubted, or they were coming for her later, which seemed the more plausible option of the two. The lust that had shown from their eyes hadn't been doused before they'd allowed her to scramble away from them, so they had allowed her to go for their own reasons. She didn't know them, didn't know how their minds worked, but she doubted that there was any charitable reasoning behind allowing her to run to freedom!

Shivering against the table jammed into the door, she stumbled into her bedroom and walked to her closet. Reaching for a thick cardigan, she wrapped herself in the swathes of cloth and hoped that the warmth would seep into her cold bones. The day had been warm so she'd worn very little today, tight jeans meant for spring weather and not the heavy-duty ones she usually wore for winter, and a small strappy vest top that left her shoulders and upper back bare. At this moment in time, though, she couldn't remember ever feeling so cold, and, as she repeated her stumbling walk to the living room, she clambered towards the picture window, ducking when she saw the three men crouched low on the ground not far from her home, still engaged in a heated argument. Although it had obviously cooled down, they appeared to be discussing something. She could only hope it wasn't about her, but that she also doubted profusely. A blush stung her cheeks as she noticed the hard cocks between their legs, something she was amazed she'd missed earlier. They were the most masculine men she had ever seen. She was surprised when she realized that those hard-ons were for her, that lust glittering away like gold dust in their eyes had been for her. So yes, they had to still be discussing her.

Dropping to her knees, she leaned her chin on the windowsill to peer out and watch them. Apparently they'd come to some sort of decision, they were now standing and looking at each other fiercely. With a frown she watched then gasped in horror as the onyx-haired man bent down and charged the man with caramel colored hair, his shoulder gouging deep into the other man's stomach.

Her hand curled into a fist, and she pushed it into her mouth to hush the moans of dismay as each man fought the other viciously. Tears welled in her eyes as signs of pain flashed on their faces. She watched in horror as they bit and scratched, tugged at hair, and punched low in the gut or kicked out in vulnerable places. This was fighting dirty, and it was a shock to her innocent eyes. Such a feral attack was unimaginable, but then what more could she expect? Mere moments ago, they had been animals, had stood before her as wolves. They *were* animals, or at least partly animal. They would therefore fight accordingly, this was obviously a normal way to fight for them.

Quickly rubbing the tears away from her eyes, she ground the heel of her hand against her left ear as one of them cried out in pain, loud enough for her to hear it as far away as she was, through the walls of her home. The sound was monstrous to her, but despite herself she couldn't help but watch them. The scene repulsed her, but couldn't tear her gaze away from them. Her body wouldn't budge from this position. Her mind yelled at her, yelled to run away and hide from these strange men, but she was glued to the spot and when she watched them transform into the wolves she'd first seen, she realized why she hadn't been able to move away. Somehow she had known they would turn into wolves, had instinctively felt it and she had had to see it once more, had to have it confirmed once more to know that it wasn't just her imagination.

As wolves, the fight grew even more, impossibly, vicious. The snarls and growls were louder now, they shuddered their way through her frame, worked their way into her system and made every single hair on her body stand on edge. She watched as the aggression unbelievably turned up a notch, in fact, more than a notch. She saw one of them jump back with a whimper, a huge jagged gash along his side. Blood poured from the angry wound, and she grimaced sympathetically but watched on in shock as his body quickly contorted in that way she now recognized and the man appeared, checking his injury. Before she could even blink, though, he was a wolf once more. She gasped in shock as the once blood-gushing wound appeared to be nothing more than a scratch, a painful looking scratch, but far less fatal than before, having healed almost entirely in moments. Obviously they healed faster than humans did. She'd never seen anything like that in all of her scientific career.

It was obviously still painful though as she watched him sort of hop on his back legs slightly, as though accustoming himself to the pain, before he leapt back into the fray and started biting into one of the others.

Seeing the transformation once more brought the scientist in her to life again. Because they were these wolf-men, or whatever the hell they were called, did that mean that her pheromone did work? But only on regular wolves and not them? Snorting at her terminology, before today she hadn't known any other kind of wolf had existed!- she frowned in thought. Blinding herself to the viciousness of the fight before her, she contemplated whether or not the pheromone actually worked.

As usual, where the pheromone was concerned, her concentration focused on the matter at hand. It had worked on the other wolves perfectly, and they were all it was supposed to work on! Not creatures out of a paranormal romance novel! Nodding her head stoutly, she realized that all her tests and predictions had been right, the trial had been a success. The only three anomalies were the ones trying to kill each other out there in front of her cabin.

Something tweaked at her memory, and, with a jolt, her gaze returned to the fight. The spray had leaked some of the liquid on to her hand. Eyes flaring wide open, she wondered if that was why they had been so attracted to her.   Despite herself, a grimace of disappointment fluttered over her face before the scientist's interest kicked into high gear. Did they lust after her because of the chemical or was it truly her they were attracted to?   The memory of their hard cocks flashed into her mind. There was no reason why the pheromone should work on their human side. There was a fifty percent chance that they were attracted because of the pheromone and a fifty percent chance that it was her.

Scowling at the thought, she asked herself why the hell it mattered.   It wasn't like she was even considering sleeping with them, was it? With these men that weren't even human? She wasn't possibly considering it . . . .

Was she?

Chapter Two

The gash had sliced its way down the entirety of his torso. Blood oozed ceaselessly from the nasty wound and every single movement seemed to rip the torn slit even further open. Even though shifting was dangerous when wounded, it was common practice during a challenge, and he instinctively knew there was no other option open to him. In this form, he couldn't see the extent of the wound, but he knew how it felt. This was bad. It was a killing blow, and Caden knew it. Mentally preparing himself for the pain, he started the transformation and dropped to his knees as agony traversed its way around his system, seeming like thousands of millions of fire ants were crawling their way around his body. Some slow and some fast, they nevertheless managed to get into every crevice, every nook and cranny in his body touched by that trail of fiery pain.

Panting heavily, he managed to suck a deep breath into his gasping lungs, grimacing angrily as his damaged ribs protested the painful jarring displacement. On a grunt, he managed to clamber to his feet. It was a struggle and he had to clutch his side all the while. Then once standing, he rubbed a hand down his injury, hissing as his callused hands rubbed against the raw, tender skin. With a sigh of relief, he noted that the gash had closed over during the shift. The blood had stopped oozing and although tender, he was once more match-ready. Automatically he returned to his wolf state and with squinted eyes looked for an entry into Dante and Shane's one on one battle.

He was getting tired, but then so were Dante and Shane. Shane had been right earlier when he'd said they were too even to fight. No one could win this challenge, and, as much as it pissed him off, he knew that. It didn't stop him from jumping back into the fray with a howl, body rigid, his ears pointing straight to the sky displaying his anger and annoyance to the other two.

Butting his head against Dante's side in a classic diversionary move, he immediately dove down and reached low to nip at the other wolf's hind leg and dragged it with him on his retreat. The diversion worked. On an uncomprehending growl, Dante fell on to his side and hindquarters with a jerk that worked aggressively through his body. Although he quickly scrambled to his feet, the maneuver had obviously weakened his shoulder as he started to hop forward on a limp then, after consideration, retreated to shift.

Although it was a challenge where anything really went so long as at the end of it there was one winner, all three men had unconsciously allowed each other to shift during the fight to heal. As Alphas, they were equally matched. Ordinarily there would be some heavy differences between wolves taking part in a challenge, one would have strengths where the other had a weakness and vice versa. Dante, Shane, and Caden, however, had been practically raised together. They had fought and played with each other since being pups, and there was no way they could exploit a weakness without their own being used against them and without the other two knowing what was happening. It was pretty impossible really, all three of them had basically just torn into each other at the start, hoping to rip and bite and tear to injure, which was working, but not enough for one of them to concede defeat or gain enough ground to win the challenge. They were working on the hope that fighting dirty enough would give one the opportunity to claim the prize.

Shane rounded on him this time, snarling aggressively, his teeth bared. Caden responded in turn. The two circled each other for a moment before Shane pounced. Caden dove quickly, realizing his intention a split-second before he made the attack and rolled out of the way, leaving Shane to crash land to the ground. Yelping in pain, Shane immediately shifted on the ground to reset his leg, unknowingly giving Dante the opportunity to attack Caden once more.

On seeing Caden roll out of the way, Dante pounced atop him and proceeded to rip the gash on his torso wide open. Simultaneously Caden bit at Dante's leg, pulling at his weakened shoulder, and, with a surprised snarl, his leg buckled, and he fell against Caden. The two of them shifted immediately to heal their dangerous wounds.

All three of them lay wounded on the ground, each panting through the pain and clutching at their injuries. On a wheezing grunt, Caden launched himself into a seating position, the lance of pain that shot its way down his side made him clench his eyes shut in agony. "Fuck that hurt," he groaned roughly, his arm clenched tightly about his waist. "Dante, you bastard," he said on a grimace before turning to give the other man a knowing, gloating look, "You do that way too often, man. You always leave your hind legs open to attack. That's twice I attacked and won."

"Fuck you," Dante responded easily, knowing his friend was right and that he'd have to work on that. "As if you don't leave your torso wide open. That Beta sliced through you, and we managed to as well. Twice, I might add." Flipping him the bird, Dante flopped back on to the ground and grunted as it jarred his aching but healing shoulder.

"I told you a challenge wouldn't work," Shane replied in an I-told-you-so tone of voice. Absently he massaged the skin around his knee, shifting had righted the broken bone, but it certainly hadn't taken the ache away.

"I didn't see you coming up with another solution. The challenge might not have worked, but we all know it was necessary," Dante answered resolutely.

"Necessary, how? To prove that we're too evenly matched? I didn't need to bust my leg for us to realize that. We know each other far too well to fight in a challenge. We all know the injuries we've got, where to attack . . . . It was a pointless exercise and probably has only managed to make *my,*" Shane emphasized the word on a hiss, "mate even more frightened of me. She's probably in that damned cabin passed out on the goddamn floor."

"It was necessary, fuck-wit, because all three of us were reacting to her pheromones. The fight has dispelled the fog, and we can now not only think clearly, but we can determine what we're going to do. This is no ordinary situation. Three Alphas who, it looks like, are going to be sharing a mate?" he said before issuing a laugh that lacked amusement. "The Fates are fucking with us. Look at Caden before the challenge. Have you ever seen him like that before?" he said, not waiting for a reply as he continued. "No, Shane, you haven't. The challenge reiterated that all three of us deserve a shot with her. Caden's wolf will have calmed down because he busted your leg and fucked with my shoulder. The challenge has played its part. The rest of this sorry farce is going to be up to us!"

"You're right. I've never felt like that before, Dante, I don't know what the fuck was going on, but he's right, Shane, all of our wolves had to be shown that we're equal. As unhappy as I am about the prospect of sharing her, I think we're going to either have to let her choose from one of us, or we're all going to have to claim her and just ride roughshod over her feelings, which I'm not crazy about. But as a wolf, sharing a mate is unusual but not completely unheard of. In the human world, it's a more than bizarre lifestyle choice, those sort of relationships are not looked upon highly. It's more than likely that she'll choose between us," he ended on a weary sigh.

"Look, none of us know what's going on here, but we all scented that crazy scent that was coming from that she-wolf. Maybe it's that, maybe it's the scent we're attracted to," Shane added a little hopefully.

Dante snorted, "The woman had that crazy scent all over her hands. If that's all you could smell then she isn't your mate." Ignoring the other man's growl of annoyance, he said, "For fuck's sake, Shane, surely you realized that was a fake pheromone. Where's your brain? Let me guess," he joked, "down by your cock."

"The she-wolf was covered in that stuff. I could scent it on the woman, but it wasn't overly pervading like the wolf," Caden informed him.

"Exactly, she's obviously experimenting with pheromones, and, apparently, she's hit the jackpot. If it attracted us as well as the natural wolves, that's a pretty damned close to natural pheromone. I didn't realize until I got closer, that that fake stuff was all over her hands, the real scent was from her and fuck, was it potent," Dante admitted, grimacing. "Because we all reacted to it in the same way, by thinking with our dicks, we've managed to scare the shit out of her. It won't be easy to coax her to like us now. Not only that, but we have to be careful. Another wolven could be attracted to the pheromone she's got on her hands. It's strong stuff. At least you two jerks believe she's your mate. I'm not sharing her with some bastard who happens to like the fake pheromone!"

"It won't be too difficult to coax her round," Shane amended. "But if we're her mates, then she's ours, and she won't be unaffected by us. She'll be wary at first. Bu who the hell wouldn't be! But she'll come around. If we keep her in the cabin with us, she'll be safe. But you're right, until that pheromone wears off, we have to be careful."

"So, what's the plan?" Caden asked.

"We'll just have to talk it through with her. There's nothing more we can do. Come on, better get it over and done with," Dante said with resolve. Grunting and clasping his shoulder, he got to his feet and waited for the other two to join him.

The there of them walked together towards the cabin and over to the door.

"I heard her lock it earlier. But maybe she's unlocked

it by now?" Shane asked no one in particular, ever hopeful. But the look on his face told a different story as he wiggled the doorknob to find the door bolted against them.

Despite themselves, despite having just competed in a challenge, and despite not wanting to frighten their mate even more, it was hard to contain the wolf against this blatant retreat. The beast inside of them wanted its mate, wanted to surround itself in her scent, wanted to be touched and touch her soft giving, womanly body, wanted to revel in the feel of her flesh against its own. That their mate had locked them out made an already bad situation worse. It was hard to contain a beast that wanted to rip down the door, fuck its mate until she was drenched in his scent, and it in hers, and forever hide her from the eyes of any other males. Her locking them out didn't ease that need at all! It forcefully called it to the fore.

Clenching his eyes closed against his beast's demand to shift, Caden grunted, "Why did she have to do that?" Twisting his neck quickly from side to side, he smiled in satisfaction as it cracked. "I could just fight that challenge again, fuck."

Dante gave a shaky laugh. "I don't blame her for having done it. I just wish she hadn't. Fuck, I never knew how badly my wolf wanted its mate."

The other two nodded in reluctant agreement.

With a sigh, Dante knocked on the door, and in the softest, most gentle voice he could manage at the moment, shouted, "Lady, please let us in. We're not going to hurt you. You don't have to be afraid."

There was silence for a few moments. It was Shane's turn to feel the need to shift as he muttered, concern evident in his voice, "Where the fuck is she? You don't think she *has* passed out, do you? We must have scared her more than we realized." The need to go and care for his mate ripped through his heart, sent a pain to wring his gut. With wide eyes filled with worry, he banged angrily on the door, "Open the door, dammit!"

They were met with nothing but silence. After a few

minutes, though, there was a soft quavering voice that came from the other side of the door.

"Go away. I don't want to be raped."

"Fuck," Caden hissed. It was getting harder and harder to hold his beast back. "Please listen. I would rather you knifed me straight in the gut than even for a second let you think I would rape you. Please, please open the door. We need to talk to you."

"You'll hurt me. I saw you fighting out there! You chased me . . . as . . . as wolves. Oh God, I'm insane. I just watched you turn into wolves and try to kill each other." The thread of panic in her voice was getting louder. Shane banged on the door again, but it just made her voice quaver even more. "I don't want to die. Please go away. Please leave me alone. I-I'll call the police. Go away!"

Dante raised his nose slightly to scent the air before whispering to the other two, "She's directly behind the door. I think she's watching us through the peep-hole. She hasn't gone for a phone to call for help. That can only be a good sign, right?" Then to her, he said quietly, "We just want to talk to you. Won't you let us in? We swear we won't harm you."

"T-talk now if you have to. I can hear you just fine from here. What do you want to tell me?"

"Okay," Dante said, inhaling deeply and begging his beast for patience and for all the Gods to grant him it! The last thing he needed was for his wolf to take him into a partial shift while he was trying to gentle his mate! "Let's start with your name."

"My name is E-Emma."

He had to admit that he was shocked she had responded at all. He'd fully expected her to ignore him. Maybe Shane was right, if she affected them so strongly, then surely they would affect her too. If they handled her calmly, perhaps she would begin to respond to them the way they wanted her to. It was only natural for her to fear them. Hell, she'd just learned that 'werewolves' existed. It was no small wonder that she thought she was insane. It killed him not to go to her, to console her, but her well-being, both physical and mental, was more important than his own needs.

"Emma. Thank you. If you'd just take a look through your peep-hole, I can introduce us. My name is Dante, I've got black hair. Shane is blond, and Caden has the brown hair. All three of us would never harm you, okay? What happened today," he said, hesitating for a moment as he debated how to continue, "We're known amongst our own kind as Wolven. You probably think we're werewolves, which I suppose in a way we are, but we prefer the term wolven. It means that we can live as easily as a human as we can as a wolf. It's part of our genetic make-up. We were born with the ability to shift. It's passed down from parent to child. We're not dangerous, and we would never hurt you, alright?" He knew he was repeating himself, but if he said it often enough, maybe she'd come to believe him.

Silence reigned on the other side of the door.

He continued softly, "Wolven are very lucky, Emma. Not only are we gifted with the powers to transform into a wolf, but upon our birth, the Fates choose a person for each and every wolven. That person is their soul mate, their other half. We spend our entire lives searching for that person and sometimes we find that mate where you least expect her, which can be a shock to the system," he said, pausing a second to let her digest that before quietly asking, "Do you understand what I'm saying, Emma?"

"Y-you're saying that you think that I'm your mate, right?"

"Yes, that's what I'm saying, and I don't think it, I know it," he replied calmly.

"You . . . you're crazy," she whispered.

"No, Emma I'm not and neither are you. This is real, but I understand that you're going to find it hard to believe me, and whatever you may think about me, I need you to believe this. I, like Caden and Shane, would rather die than harm one single hair on your head. If you believe nothing else, know that what I'm saying now is the truth," he answered softly.

"I'm frightened," she mumbled, more to herself than to him. "This can't be happening, not now. I'm so close, the trials . . . . Why now?"

"Look, Emma, just open the door and we can discuss this rationally face to face," Caden pleaded, fully aware that she wasn't likely going to do as he requested. Then looking at Dante, who looked at Shane, each man nodded his head and with grim determination faced the door. "Stand clear, Emma," Caden called out, then rushed the door with his shoulder. The bang was unearthly in the otherwise silent forest. The shocked scream of fright behind the door wasn't exactly pleasant either.

As Caden moved away, Dante stood with his side to the door, lifting a leg, he rested it against the panel, then hovering above it for a second, he inhaled deeply, and, using the core strength from his thighs and torso, he kicked the locked door, once, twice, and the lock buckled.

Shane rushed it with his shoulder. This time the door swung open, and each man took a step through the door, ready to claim what belonged to them.

They were still naked. They were still gorgeous. And, according to them, she was their soul mate.

She couldn't even begin to understand what was happening here. She felt as though she'd fallen down the rabbit hole and had come out the other side with a severe concussion.

They'd told her that the Fates had created her for them. What was she supposed to say to that? How could she tell them that it wasn't her they were attracted to but the pheromone? A pheromone she had created with the express purpose of creating attraction where none was normally found? They believed the Fates had chosen her as theirs, and it seemed there was no way in hell that they were going to believe anything else.

And despite herself, a tiny part of her really liked

their answer, perversely wished that it wasn't the
pheromone at work here. She knew there wasn't a
possibility that it wasn't the pheromone, but, even with
it, how could these three men want *her*? It seemed
impossible and totally unlikely. No matter how
depressing it was. She knew that they were attracted
to the pheromone, and she couldn't let herself forget
that, even if she wanted to. If she started to believe
what they were telling her, then it would break her
heart at the end when they learned the truth and
realized Emma wasn't who they thought she was,
wasn't their soul mate. It was best to err on the side of
caution-yeah, where you've always stayed. But
suddenly the rogue thought fluttered through her mind
that she had always played it cautious, tried to stay
safe, and just look where that had gotten her. She was
now twenty-nine years old, she lived alone, she was
obsessed with her work, and she hadn't had a
boyfriend since she couldn't remember when.

Insidious thoughts, thoughts that she longed with all
her heart to believe, flittered through her mind. What
if they were right? What if the Fates had chosen her
for them? What if that was why they wanted her?
What if they *were* meant to be together? What if she
fit in with them like she did with her wolves? What if
she did belong with them?" She clenched her eyes
tightly shut against the errant thoughts because they
weakened her resolve, and right now she couldn't
afford to let that happen.

She had to admit that when the door crashed open
and the three bare-assed men walked into her small
house, that her resolve completely flew out of the
window. They looked at her with such intent and such
feeling that it made her heart flutter uncertainly, and
she staggered backwards in shock, trying to get away
from them. She clenched a hand when she heard the
growl that escaped one of their throats and
instinctively knew that she'd displeased them by
moving away from them. But they'd frightened her,
she thought indignantly. They'd just broken down her

door, and they expected her to be alright with that? With a scowl she opened her mouth to ask them what the hell was going on, but instead her gaze took control of her senses, and she focused on the black-haired one, the one who had said his name was Dante, his gaze turning from fear to hunger.

Her eyes blurred slightly as she studied his face. He was one of the most beautiful men she had ever seen. Although she didn't think he led these other two men. They were all too strong and powerful in their own right and didn't seem to be led by anyone. In fact if these men that claimed to be what they had informed her was wolven followed the same lifestyle patterns of natural wolves, then she was sure they were all Alpha males.

Although she sensed that Dante had an aura of menacing power surrounding him, she thought about how he'd acted when he'd been behind the door, how he'd tried to be fair and considerate, and yet always in control. She felt certain anyone who met him wouldn't, couldn't say no to this man, unless it was what he wanted. With just one look she could see that he wasn't a man who you could push and get away with it.

His hair was pitch black, as dark as she had ever seen hair. It was cut short at the sides, but it was longer on top, and when he ran impatient fingers through his hair, it stuck up in an attractive way that framed his masculine face to perfection. His forehead was broad, his eyebrows dark slashes on his face beneath which lay piercing golden brown eyes that flashed intensely at her. His nose long and straight, his lips lush and a deep rose color, his jaw was narrow but strong, raising his cheekbones to delicious prominence. With a gulp, her gaze followed the line of his jaw to his neck which was corded with tendons, continued down his body to see pecs sprinkled with hair over the center of his chest and dusted his nipples. She noticed that his pecs bulged as if he was restraining himself, but couldn't stop to think about that, couldn't stop herself from examining him further. A thin trail of hair followed the central line of his eight-pack, and she had the sudden longing to follow that path with her mouth, to press a blaze of kisses down those delicious inches of skin.

The trail stopped before the deep brown hair dusting his navel and meandered down over his pubic bone. Her eyes closed as they began the long walk up his erection, her pussy clenching at the thought of that hard cock invading her, because it would be an invasion, that she knew. There was nothing soft about any of these men. Perhaps they did believe that she was their mate, she could see it in their eyes, and it frightened her to death!

She immediately remembered the other two that were standing beside him, and her eyes trailed to the blond, the one Dante had called Shane. His hair was a little longer than Dante's, not overly so, but a lustrous combination of blonds that any woman would have killed for and would only be able to achieve at the most expensive hair salons. Dusky brownish blonds combined with sunshine-tinted white streaks, strawberry blonds blended with gold. The mixture suited the color of his flesh and added to his attraction a thousand-fold. A light but attractive tan touched every inch of his body, which was dusted with the more dark and golden blonds like the ones on his head. His stomach, although toned and muscled, was less prominent than Dante's, his waist thicker, but with no spare inch anywhere. The dark blonde hair that dusted his navel invited her gaze to look elsewhere. She heard him laugh when her gaze alighted on his cock, causing her to nearly snap her neck in her haste to look back at his face. Her mouth watered at the shocking emerald green eyes that flashed lustfully at her, the almost pretty face that was far too masculine to describe with such a feminine adjective. She examined his mouth, there was no evidence of the laugh from a moment before. His mouth was delicious, set in a strong jaw as it was. Attractive dark blond stubble coated the lower half of his face and was a complete contrast to his almost hairless chest which glinted in the sunlight and added to the masculinity his body seemed to exude.

The other man moved restlessly beside Dante, drawing her gaze to him. Dante had called him Caden. He was equally as attractive, in his own way even more so. His skin was a deep olive color, golden flesh that rippled and bulged with muscles during movement. Every inch of him was smooth yet hard, his flesh seemed soft but tightly packed as it was with muscle. She knew that the softness was an illusion. She knew that when her hand trailed along the length of his torso, she would feel hard steel beneath the velvet of his skin. His pecs weren't prominent, neither were his stomach muscles, but it suited him. But none of this hid the strength he possessed, which was obvious to the eye. All three were tall, far taller than her, Caden being the smallest of the three, his body slightly more narrow. It seemed like an optical illusion, because she'd seen him fight, had watched as his body flexed and his muscles contracted. Everything about him exuded power and strength. He may have been slightly smaller than the other two, but that intriguing power lay dormant behind his golden flesh, and it would be a huge mistake to underestimate this man. Even she could see that and she had never been in a fight in her life! His hair was a deep dark brown, but not to be mistaken for Dante's black hair. It had such a silken texture that she could almost imagine it brush against her inner thighs and the thought made her shudder. It would be soft not coarse, wonderful to the touch, yet the style itself was no-nonsense and easy to maintain, just a simple short back and sides, very military. His dark brown eyes glinted in the sunlight as he devoured her with his hungry gaze. Almost black, the density was unusual, and she felt as though she could drown in the lush orbs. Like the other two, his jaw was strong, his face utterly masculine, but so beautiful it made her heart want to weep.

It seemed incredible, make that impossible, that these three men actually wanted her. It actually made her shake her head in surprise, but the fact that they did indeed want her was even obvious to her, the usually oblivious woman in a white lab coat! The hard proof, as it were, stood in front of her wide gaze, and, God help her, she wanted them, wanted that leashed power to be freed upon her, longed to feel their strength overpower her and take her somewhere she'd never been before. It both frightened and disconcerted her that she could feel so much for three men she didn't even know, men that weren't even men.

"What do you want?" she asked huskily then almost kicked herself. She sounded positively eager for their attentions! How pathetic could she possibly be? What was going on with her?

Dante answered her question simply and very effectively, "You."

"You said you wouldn't rape me," she accused him, although her voice was hesitant, she was daring him to renege on his earlier statement.

"We won't. I've told you before, we would never harm you," he answered with what patience he could muster under the circumstances, then continued, "But look deep inside yourself Emma. Look for the real you and ask yourself, would we need to rape you?"

She was surprised at the direction his retort had taken. She frowned but realized that he was correct. It most definitely would not be rape. She didn't have to look all that far to realize that her body was eager and her mind, surprisingly, was too. Swallowing nervously, she placed her hand protectively around her neck, looked down, and whispered, "I've never done anything like this before."

"Are you a virgin?" Dante asked, trying to keep his voice calm and soothing. Her downcast eyes didn't enable her to see the flash of triumph in his eyes, nor the strong shadow of possession that quickly followed.

"I . . . I . . . ," she hesitated, her eyes clenched shut nervously at the intimacy of the question. What kind of question was that anyway? She never discussed that sort of thing with anyone, not that she had girlfriends to talk to about it. Sure, she'd never been prolific with men, but she wasn't a cringing virgin either. She'd just always had more important things in her life to tend to besides men. They'd always taken a backseat to her work. She had a feeling, though, that if any of the men she'd been with had been special, they wouldn't have fallen by the wayside.

"There's no need to be nervous, my mate," Caden replied, his voice a little hoarse with the need. His voice told its own story, like Dante thrills of possession and triumph coursed their way like quicksilver throughout his veins. That his mate could be basically untouched was more than his wolf could stand.

She gave a small nod and whispered, "I'd rather not talk about it."

"Do you want us, Emma?" Shane asked roughly.

All three of them were hanging by a thread for her answer.

She didn't seem to realize it. With a helpless shrug, she nodded again and answered quietly but honestly, "I'm scared."

"We will take care of you, Emma, this I promise you. You have no need to fear us, no need at all. Your pleasure is our pleasure, and your pleasure is all that matters to us. Believe that, my mate," Dante said as he strode confidently over to her. He held out his hand for hers.

She gave it to him cautiously. Did she really have any other choice? She was surrounded by three powerful men. It wasn't as if she could stop them even if she wanted to. She felt her cheeks flame, though, because she knew she didn't want to stop them. Wasn't his what every girl wanted? To have men look at you as if you were the only woman in the world.

He covered her hand and wrapped her small delicate fingers within his rough callused palm.

Just thinking about that strong hand smoothing over her breasts, along her inner thigh made her tremble inside, that that one simple touch could set such a fire alight inside her body, shook her to the depths of her being. Nerves overtook her, fear for what might happen in the future made her resolve to enjoy these moments, to enjoy these men because what they were offering could come only once in a lifetime. What they offered her here was pleasure beyond her wildest imaginings. How could she forgo a night in their arms? The simple answer was, she couldn't.

Pausing a second, she turned back and asked a little hesitantly, "But what about the front door?"

"No one will come in, but, Shane, place the door against the jamb. The illusion of a closed door is better than nothing at all."

Smiling up at him gratefully, he tugged her hand and led her into her bedroom.

With a shaky sigh, her gaze lowered to the floor, she asked a little uncomfortably, "I . . . I . . . . What do we do now?"

"We pleasure you, my dearest mate," Caden replied gruffly, obviously hearing her question as he walked through the door, his body ready for the hours ahead.

"We?" she squeaked.

"Yes," Dante said, sounding amused. "You'll enjoy it, I promise."

She didn't have anything to say to that. She enjoyed just looking at them, how could she not enjoy being intimate with them? She blew out a nervous breath as she stood beside her bed, anxiously fiddling with her fingers, twining them and flexing them while she waited for them to do something.

Dante walked up to her. Putting a finger underneath her chin, forcing her to look at him, he whispered, "I've told you, there's no need to be nervous, sweeting." Having said that, he leaned down and pressed a tender kiss to her lips. It started out as a kiss that cherished, that was thankful and grateful to have found her, but as his mouth softly began to explore

Emma's, nipping at the Cupid's bow of her lips, licking gently at her bottom lip, that cherishing kiss turned into a display of mastery.

His soft explorations both gentled and aroused her until, unable to help it, she began to moan eagerly against his mouth, opening her own to accept his questing tongue. Although it wasn't her first kiss, it felt like the first time anyone had ever pressed their lips to hers, and, she thought, a little dazedly, that every woman deserved a Dante for their first kiss. To say that he was treating her like spun glass was an understatement. Behind every little touch was a desire to inspire and enhance passion, and it worked.

She jumped a little in surprise as she felt another mouth make contact with her skin, felt it explore the sensitive nape of her neck. She arched into Dante's hard frame as the hands of the man behind her started to smooth their way up her waist to cup her breasts. The soft trail of a tongue along her shoulders made her tremble. Squashed as she was between them, the pressure of two hard cocks against her butt and hip made her squirm. Dante's mouth started to work against hers, faster and faster, until his tongue began thrusting into the dark crevice of her mouth. He began to fuck with his tongue and a wash of excitement flowed over her, making her feel weak in the knees, making her weak all over. Panting now against his mouth, she was desperate to touch him and reached up and pressed her hands against his hard pecs. Her fingers curled against them, her nails raking the hard flesh as he masterfully ratcheted her excitement up tenfold with the play of his tongue in her mouth. That just a kiss could inspire such need, could create such an intense desire was incredible to her.

With another jolt of surprise, she felt a man's hands tugging on the fly of her pants, felt and heard the slow slide of the zipper. As his fingers trailed down the front panel of her panties, she groaned her arousal against Dante's mouth. Now aching with the need that was consuming her body, she reared her head back to angle her head to better receive the other man's kisses. It was Caden, she discovered when she turned to look, who immediately took advantage of her position and began to penetrate her mouth with his tongue, stroking against hers at the same tempo as his fingers stroked her through her panties, stroked her first slowly then at a quickened pace.

His fingers trailed down her body, down until they touched her more intimately.

She stiffened against this new sensation but relaxed again as she felt the tenderness behind his every action. His fingers just rested there, as though waiting for her acceptance. When one long digit slid down the center of her pussy, she could feel her body working, could feel the slow slippery juices escaping to coat her panties. One finger slid underneath the feeble shield of her panties and the protesting whimper that escaped her throat was muffled against his mouth.

Her body tensed at so intimate a touch, and when Dante's hands slid underneath her t-shirt and eventually underneath her bra, she groaned as he cupped then teased and tweaked her eager nipples. The dual caresses made her responses increase instantly, to be touched in such a different way and in two separate erogenous zones, made her feel as if an avalanche of sensation was sweeping over her and dragging her under.

Caden ran one finger teasingly along the edge of her pussy lips, the movement slow and easy.

It worked her body in the opposite way. It made her desire even more urgent, her need for their touch seeming to take over her body.

Somehow it was necessary that they both touched her, that both worked together for her pleasure. Knowing that they both watched her, both felt her, both worked to please her only served to increase her desire until she was panting to breathe, her lungs unable to take in enough air to cope with the onslaught of feeling.

Opening her eyes, she looked deep into Caden's gaze

as their tongues tangled and as his finger pressed against her weeping flesh forcefully until she lost all sight, closing her eyes to revel in the feelings their touch elicited.

She shuddered then jerked in shock as Dante whispered gruffly, "Don't tease her, Caden."

Having said that, he grabbed Caden's hand and pulled it away from her then returned his hands to her body where he proceeded to slowly peel her T-shirt away from her tingling skin. Unfastening the clasp on her bra, he released her breasts in to the palms of his hands and allowed Caden to remove the offending material.

Caden then dropped to his knees and pulled her jeans down over her hips and thighs; his hands returning to her panties, he tugged at them, allowing them to drop to the floor to lay in a puddle with her trousers. She stood dazedly all the while as they worked to free her from her clothes, half-blind half-deaf with the tumult of feeling that was bombarding her.

Standing naked, sandwiched, between two men should perhaps have frightened her, but instead thrills of adrenaline rushed their way throughout her body. Where she touched them, where their flesh met, she felt burning tingles of arousal and a faint sheen of sweat covered her body. Dante pressed himself against her and instinctively her back arched against his as she felt the first touch of his velvet cock brush against the soft yielding skin of her belly. A powerful shudder of lust trembled along her nerves, as he then lowered his hands and cupped her butt, lifting her away from her clothes and walking her to her bed. She clung to him as he turned away from the bed and sat on the edge before lowering himself backwards so that he lay flat on his back with her somewhat awkwardly pressed against him.

His eyes flashed at hers warmly, tenderly, lovingly and he murmured, "Crawl over me." With a frown of confusion, she sat up and spread her legs to kneel against the bed, but did as he asked, crawling over him until her pussy brushed against his cock. He shook his head and whispered, "I want your pussy here," tapping a finger against his mouth, she shuddered when she realized what he wanted her to do. Emma eagerly complied with his wishes, ignoring the nerves that threatened to strike at her confidence as she awkwardly moved along his body.

It was rather difficult crawling over his torso, but she had the feeling that he wanted her to slide over his chest, she herself felt the wetness of her juices brush along his skin and saw the flash of lust in his eyes as he felt it too. To manage the maneuver, she had to bend over and lean against her arms, which dropped her breasts, making them dangle like earrings in his face. Upon reaching his upper torso, she literally had to drag herself along his body and gave a small sigh of relief as his hands came up and cupped her butt, aiding her by lifting her up and over so that when her knees once more settled against the bed, her pussy was directly over his face.

The thought made her shudder, the wash of his breath against so sensitive an area made her tremble and her eyes thanked Caden as he walked over towards the bed and allowed her to lean against him. Curving his neck slightly, he whispered, "I'll be your support throughout your life, mate." Her eyes widened in surprise at this unexpected statement, but he shook his head as though to ward off a reply and he continued, "Enjoy his touch, Emma." He smiled knowingly as a blush spread over her cheeks and as the tendons in her neck began to stand out in prominence.

That first long glide of his tongue down the center of her cunt was Emma's first indication that she was totally out of her depth here. As it wiggled low and pressed into the entrance of her body, the feeling of that boneless flexible muscle made her pussy clench hard as though trying to catch it. He allowed her no control however and soon his tongue was sweeping upwards and brushing her clit in light fluttery strokes.

Suddenly she was more than grateful for Caden's support, she was desperate for it, wouldn't have been able to manage without him there to help her. Sinking against his broad chest, her head cushioned by a pec, Caden cupped her waist, holding her straight so as not to suffocate Dante. Her need for support changed the way they touched, suddenly his hard skin pressed against hers, his erect cock dug into her belly and she could literally feel the tremors every now and then, all these sensations merely added to her arousal until she felt almost insensate. Every single inch of her felt hyper-sensitized and over-ready, the tongue that was flicking her clit only enhanced every sensation, making her muscles alternately clench and tense in readiness, then release and sag as the intensity of her arousal finally caught up to her.

Without really thinking, without contemplating why, her hand reached out for Caden's cock. There was no hesitance in her touch, she wrapped the pulsing muscle in her fist tightly and gave a low groan at the feel of it against the palm of her hand. She had no real idea of what to do to please him until his hips began to pump and with a shaky sigh, she moved her hand up and down, clenching him as tightly as she possibly could along the way. Her other hand reached downwards for his balls, she fisted him there as well, her body telling her instinctively that it would please him. Her eyes flashed up to his and she was pleased to see the desire and intense lust she felt, reflected in his own. It was wonderful knowing that she wasn't alone in this heightened situation, that he and probably Dante felt exactly the same as she. Emma had the feeling that he wouldn't allow himself to climax in her hand, didn't know how she knew that, but it still gave her pleasure to feel him pulse against her fingers, to feel his response to her touch in such a tactile manner. There was something honest about their caresses and presence and it easily allowed her to come to terms with the depth of feeling they inspired in her.

Abruptly the bed shuddered, and she realized that Shane must have returned to the bedroom after fixing the door somehow. Resting her cheek upon Caden's chest, she gave a small sigh as Dante began to fuck her with his tongue, her hips began to rock in earnest now and sliding her head around to look for Shane, a flash of lust so strong powered through her upon seeing him with his hand around his cock, obviously enjoying the show.

Crying out in readiness, Emma felt Dante's hands cup her butt and he somehow pushed her down so that her tender flesh dragged against his face. Hissing at the feel of the stubble of chin against her entrance, she pictured the juices coating his face, her mark upon him and she shuddered as an orgasm flushed through her body, flushed through her very soul. Working its way through every inch of her system, the pleasure hit sporadically and at will, like small bombs detonating upon the surface of her skin. A loud cry escaped her throat and she sagged almost entirely against Caden, her hands releasing him as she tried to find her equilibrium but to no avail.

Those triggers of pleasure were too potent, far too strong to run away from and suddenly a smile lit up her face as she realized that now, now she knew what an orgasm felt like.

Chapter Three

Eyes clenched tightly closed, Emma allowed herself to be arranged on the bed. She didn't want to open her eyes and face what had just happened. She hated the blush that tinged her cheeks, and she wouldn't have been surprised if she discovered that it covered her entire body, coloring each of her limbs in a rosy red hue. She wasn't ashamed of what had just happened, not in the least, but she had no idea what to do next and the not knowing filled her stomach with butterflies. She'd always been in control. To be so far out of her depths, to basically have jumped in the deep end with no armbands and no real knowledge of how to swim, terrified her.

Suddenly it she became very aware of being naked with these three men looking at her. When they'd started to strip off her pants and T-shirt, she hadn't really been aware of anything but what they were doing to her, what they were making her experience, what they were making her feel. Now, however, now that they weren't assaulting her from every direction with distracting pleasurable touches, she almost felt like cringing in horror at how easily she'd capitulated to their touch. There had been some level of inevitability about the whole thing, but that didn't make it right. She felt both naked in body and in soul, and it only added to her nerves and discomfort.

She tried not to think about how her body looked, because it begged the question-were they disappointed? They thought she was their mate, did they look at her and think she was unattractive, unappealing? She knew she wasn't model material. Her breasts weren't the largest, her belly was pretty taut and her butt relatively toned, but that was only because she forgot to eat all the time because she was always so heavily intent on her work. When she did remember, she ate what she wanted, and that unfortunately ranged from fat-filled donuts to bags of chips. She knew that other women worried about cellulite. She wasn't sure if she had any, had never really bothered to look. But what if she did have cellulite? What if it her body repulsed them?

Suddenly every little body issue she'd ever had over the last twenty-nine years of her life seemed to take the forefront in her mind. It was hard to believe that this morning she'd been so uncaring of her appearance and now, within what seemed like five minutes, it had become so incredibly important to her. Perhaps having just climaxed on some guy's face while leaning against his friend and being watched by another of his pals meant that she shouldn't really be thinking about her how her thighs looked, but she couldn't help it. This wasn't something she was used to and her new body issues were only adding to worries. Was there some kind of protocol for the 'moment' after when you'd been with more than one man and none of them human? Of course, she had no idea. Was she supposed to jump up perkily and look at them lustily in wait for round two? Was she supposed to just lie there and wait for them to make the next move? She had no idea what she was she supposed to do.

Embarrassment threatened to swamp her, actually making her feel queasy in the process, and so Emma took a huge gulp of air and bravely decided to open her eyes to face the consequences.

Within a second of baring her gaze, she regretted it. Each man watched her, a powerful lust printed on their face, a need and desire for *her* stamped in their eyes. It was incredible but overwhelming, and she knew that her cheeks would once again be blooming with color at this moment. On the other hand, as her gaze glanced downwards, she felt her desire build again. Their cocks, their impossibly large cocks that were somehow supposed to fit inside her, were still hard, were ready to fuck her. So even if she did have wobbly thighs, it didn't bother them or their erections in the slightest, even if she was different from them.

As a hand trailed over her leg and rested possessively against her stomach, she squirmed at how right that touch felt and turn to look into Caden's eyes.

A soft and tender smile lit his face, and he whispered, "Don't be embarrassed, my mate." Leaning down, he nuzzled his jaw against her own.

With that simple caress, she felt a hundred times better, felt reassured and warmed by how important her comfort was to them.

There was no need to be uncomfortable with these three men. They weren't judging her, they wanted her. She had no idea how they would react if they knew how much she wanted them. She returned his comforting gesture and placed a hand atop the one on her stomach. Squeezing it softly, she pressed a kiss to his cheek.

"Open your legs, my mate," he said quietly, it wasn't an order, his voice was filled with too much emotion for it to be a demand, but he expected her to comply and like night followed day, she naturally spread her legs and clutched them tightly about his waist when he settled himself atop her. His cock brushed her pussy, but he made no move to start anything. Instead, he just rested there, the majority of his weight supported by his forearms which lay beside her head.

His chest still pressed against hers, her nipples digging into his skin and being so close to him, was so wonderfully new that she reveled in the luxuriousness of being so near this beautiful man. As he looked steadfastly into her eyes, the deep dark dense black of his eyes was so intense that she almost lost herself in his gaze, almost lost herself in him. Try as she might, though, she couldn't close her eyes against him, couldn't shut him out no matter that she wanted to. It was easier to stop the tide than it was to blank him. There was such a wealth of promise in his look that the woman in her, not the scientist, blossomed in the emotions he was transmitting. She was lost. If they broke only used her and then left her then at least she'd have experienced something in her sterile existence, she could say that she had known the intensity of need and desire even if she never had felt the slow seedlings of love take root and begin to flourish. Had she never met these men, she most likely would have died at an old age, lonely, her heart cold and hard from lack of human relationships, having never experienced the beauty of these moments, with her one possible success that she might have managed to help the world's wolf population. And, while that satisfied the scientist in her, it certainly didn't quench the woman's need.

And the woman did need. It was just that up until now, up until she'd met them, she simply hadn't realized it.

Caden bent his head down to press a soft kiss against her parted red lips.

He was gentle, but his chest against hers was abrading her pouting nipples with the slightest movement of his breathing. The slow rise and fall of his chest as he breathed gently caressed her with his hardness, and, as each second passed, her entire being began to crave his possession. Thanks to Dante, her pussy was wet and ready for Caden's cock. Each brush of his hard form against her began to drive her insane. Need seemed to stream from every pore until a slight tremor began to overtake her. She would never have imagined that such an intensity of feeling could begin the way this had, with him just laying above her, gently kissing her, touching her, absentmindedly and without direction. Perhaps that was where her urgency had come from, his seeming *lack* of urgency drove hers upwards and out of control.

The small tremors transmitted her need to him and with a small smile, he reached down to grab his cock. In a move that made her cry out, he ran the glans of his dick along the center of her pussy, coating himself in her juices for lubrication.

She didn't know why, but she craved his cock like she

craved air. The feeling of such strength running along the tenderness of her pussy made her squirm hungrily. When his cock rubbed over her clit, her back arched helplessly, her mouth parted, and her eyes clenched shut. Arousal lit a flame in her body and she couldn't douse it, and neither did she want to.

Her body moved jerkily, and for a few moments she forgot to breathe, waiting as she was for that moment when he penetrated her. Her knees moved from around his hips and instead she planted her feet on the duvet to ground herself. As the round blunt head of his cock pressed at her entrance, she tensed, her thighs clenching warily. Her stomach muscles tensed in wait until eventually she thought she'd go insane. She opened her eyes to look at him, pleading with him to ease the ache that was threatening to overtake her. His hips answered her plea, softly pressing against her, and, inch by inch, he worked himself inside her.

With a few experimental flutters, her pussy, she realized, was unsure of how to react to this intruder. At first, she pressed against him, not allowing him entrance, because suddenly the sheer size of him lit a stir of panic in her. As he started to conquer her, she began to gasp for air, leaving her feeling like a floundering fish as she'd been so uncertain as to how to coordinate herself to his movements. But, in the end, it hadn't been necessary, because feeling him filling her, that full sensation that pervaded her lower body, a luxurious sensation of rightness engulfed her. It felt so fucking right to have him there that she almost felt like weeping. Instead, another emotion took over, one that demanded he take action and pleasure her. She jerked her hips down then upwards, from left to right and begged in a voice that was suddenly a little hoarse, "Help me, Caden, please." With her head tilted backwards against the bed in sexual anguish, she didn't see the fire that ignited in his eyes at her words. A desperate need had overwhelmed her, and she didn't, she couldn't, cope with it, had no idea what to do to ease the burning desire that his cock had started.

Slowly, ever so slowly, he retreated, his cock pulling at unused tissues that made her whimper and her insides flutter. Thrusting in again, she gave a soft grunt as he went deep, his hips flush to hers, and although it almost hurt, it felt so good, so, so good, so wonderful that a mew of pleasure escaped her throat. His hips rocked faster and faster. Deeper and deeper he continued to plunge into her depths until she climaxed, her pussy quivering around his cock, milking him for everything he was worth.

When her eyes opened moments . . . what seemed like an eternity later, she looked at him blearily and whispered accusingly and with more than a little confusion, her voice throaty, "You didn't cum."

His molasses-colored eyes burned into hers as he whispered, "That's because it's not over yet, my mate."

She felt her face flame anew at his words.

He gave her a naughty smile that sent a renewed spark of excitement coursing through her tired body before shaking his head and muttering, "Do you know how beautiful that was?" Clutching her sides, he rolled over until she lay astride him.

Sitting up, she gave a low moan as his cock resettled itself inside her. Panting slightly at the fullness, she pressed her hands against his chest and wiggled a little, unused to such a feeling.

Shane moved towards her then. Placing a hand to her lower back, he placed pressure against her so that she fell forwards and against Caden. Her head whipped around when she felt her butt cheeks being spread open, but Caden reached up and cupped her face with his hands and whispered, "Enjoy yourself, my mate. We won't hurt you."

She didn't have time to say anything, she didn't have time to really think about what was happening. When a tongue fluttered against the rosette of her ass, she had to suppress the urge to squeak. She was shocked. No one had ever done that before! The sensation was . . . disturbing. It sent chills fluttering around her stomach, and a strange new desire pervaded her system. Never would she have believed that there would be so many nerve-endings down there, but, apparently there were, and Shane had managed to touch what seemed like every single one of them. A finger smoothed down the skin that joined her butt and pussy, and on a groan she shuddered as it rimmed her entrance, placing pressure against the already tightly packed area of her cunt.

Through her sexually heated fog, she thought she heard Dante say, "She had this in her bathroom cabinet." When she felt an oily finger prod at her butt hole, she realized that he must be using her petroleum jelly as a sort of lubrication, and her hips moved forward instinctively to escape the oily digit that was trying to thrust into her behind.

"Be still," Dante ordered as he clutched her butt between his hands to stop her from moving, "We have to prepare you." She stiffened at the order, but inhaled on a shuddery breath as Shane gently worked his finger inside her, then another and then another.

It was becoming harder and harder to breath. She felt so full, too full. Spread open the way she was, a sense of panic started to invade her.

"Hey, look at me," Caden murmured, seeing the trepidation in her eyes, he quickly raised his mouth to hers, tangling his tongue urgently with hers, distracting her with his hungry biting kisses that relaxed her infinitesimally, enough to allow Shane to prepare her.

When the head of a cock butted the rosette of her ass, she threw herself deeper into Caden's kiss, closed her eyes to what was happening, because she felt like she would burst if Shane actually managed to penetrate her. Her tongue twisted and twined with Caden's, passionately rekindling both their needs.

"Try to relax," Dante whispered, "It'll be easier," he pressed a kiss to her cheek, dotted them over and around her jaw line, trailed his tongue along the line of her neck, until her skin started to throb, the sheer contrast between his delicate touch, Caden's urgent kissing, and Shane's determined penetration set her on fire, set her alight with sensation until, suddenly impatient to have it over with, she rocked roughly backwards and gave a small squeal as Shane took that as acquiescence and drove his cock deep into her ass.

Panting heavily, she couldn't help but feel torn in two and pressed her head against Caden's chest, feeling some mild discomfort. A frown creased her face, and her eyes closed tight in self-defense.

"You should have taken it more slowly, Shane," Dante reprimanded him, glaring at him for a second before he went back to caressing Emma, resting his face against her neck.

Somehow, only God knew how, between Dante and Caden distracting her, they eased the feeling of total fullness. Having Dante and Caden there, and, even though he was the source of her new discomfort, having Shane there, somehow helped, and gradually, although it could have been minutes or hours, she relaxed around their cocks.

Both men grunted in relief, and Caden murmured softly into her ear, "Emma, my mate, you complete me."

With dazed eyes she looked at him. From the look in his eyes, she knew that he thought what he was saying was the truth.

Shane ruined the moment by slowly pulling free from her, which instinctively made her clutch at him, and this time all three of them groaned. Somewhere within that space of time, her body had readied itself to be fucked by them in this way. With surprise, she realized that she was actually responding to the dual penetration. As Shane pushed back in, Caden started to pull out and together they worked her into such a frenzy that she felt like bursting. Release didn't seem imminent though, it seemed somehow to be waiting, waiting for something.

Dante, seeing the tension in her face, lifted her up slightly and worked a hand between her and Caden and then between her legs.

As his fingers delicately strummed her clit, her climax suddenly didn't seem so far away. As all three men worked together to make her cum, her breath halted in her chest as a sensation so powerful engulfed her, made her drown in an explosion of pleasure, which blinded and deafened her to anything and everything around her. Her mind was black, filled with nothing. It seemed never ending, and the final push came as she felt the burst of Shane and Caden's release.

On a choked cry, she surrendered to the blackness, to the silence, to the peace.

* * * *

Perching delicately on the kitchen stool, Emma poured herself a huge bowl of cereal and drenched it in milk. Taking the huge heaping spoonful to her mouth, she swallowed with a sigh of relief. Her stomach had been her alarm clock this morning. Grumbling as though it had never been fed, she'd had to scramble out of the over-crowded bed, all the while hoping to God that the three men hadn't heard her stomach making noises and had then retreated to the kitchen for some sustenance.

She ate the first bowl ravenously and guiltily filled a second. It was strange to feel guilty over having seconds, and, with a frown she realized that ordinarily she wouldn't have given a damn, would have had fourths or even fifths if necessary, all depending on her hunger. But on remembering how she'd suddenly started to panic about her body image, she bit her lip before starting on the second bowl with a scrunched defiant face. Surely all that sex had burned a lot of calories? It meant that this one bowl of cereal didn't count, didn't it?

She could only hope so because she was damned hungry, and she refused to starve just for beauty. She'd never cared about it before, and she wasn't going to start now. What had happened between them wasn't going to change anything, because, whatever they had, whatever feelings they thought they felt, it was all going to be over as soon as the pheromone was gone. But the night before had been the first time she'd ever been completely naked in front of any man, never mind three of them, and each of them more gorgeous than Adonis. Was it any wonder that she'd been a little self-conscious? Anyway, twenty-nine years of indifference couldn't be changed overnight, she thought with a resolute nod. She may be eating seconds, but she would stop there. Before last night, that certainly wouldn't have happened, but, she told herself it wasn't because of them, it was because she wanted to.

Ignoring her thought of her body image, she ate her breakfast with enjoyment then, as a stray thought entered her head, she snorted suddenly and choked as a spoonful of cereal went down the wrong way. Coughing loudly, she quickly drank some milk to get rid of the sugary treat that felt as though it was stuck in her windpipe, and when she could breathe normally again, she dropped her face on to the counter in embarrassment. She had recalled waking up in the middle of the night, only half awake, to see Dante between her thighs, tracing and suckling her pussy lips, delving his tongue into her pussy. She'd recalled how she'd jumped in shock, but Caden had placed an arm over her stomach and cuddling up to her before whispering, "Sleep, Emma, what he's doing will heal you. Do you want to be sore tomorrow?"

Her flushed face had said, 'Yes, I would prefer that to being so intimately cleaned', but they seemed to be taking their vow to never hurting her seriously, damned seriously if you asked her! And, despite herself, the touch had been more soothing than arousing, and she'd succumbed to Dante's ministrations easily and had settled herself into Caden's arms with Shane eventually clinging to her in the night as well. At peace within their embrace, and finally relaxing after Dante had quit, she'd felt calm enough to sleep. But now, mortification filled her, and, with a grimace, she pushed her bowl away, stood up, and placed it in the sink.

She'd grabbed a T-shirt before leaving the bedroom,

and she was damned glad that she had, because on hearing the pad of footsteps on her tiled kitchen floor, a blush of discomfiture diffused over her flesh. She was so glad to be partially covered up!

"Are you okay, Emma?" It was Dante, his voice a little rough from just waking up.

She knew from her little bit of experience with them that he was the mediator in his group and that he would be with her as well. His stance was protective, as though all she had to do was tell him which dragon to slay to make her happy and he'd go and do it.

The thought made her smile and turning her head slightly to look at him, she said truthfully, "Fine, thank you." She instinctively knew that had he realized he was the cause of her mortification, it would have wounded him severely.

Tilting his head to one side in a question, he walked over to her and placed a large hand against the small of her back, when she sighed at his touch and stepped closer to be in his arms, he whispered, "Promise?"

"Yeah, just a little shell-shocked," she murmured quietly, nuzzling her cheek against his chest, both giving and receiving comfort from the non-sexual touch.

"No need to be, you're a natural," he teased harmlessly then said, "Can I have a kiss?"

Emma looked up at him with a shy but mischievous smile and nodded. Turning into his arms she had to stand on tiptoe to reach for his mouth, because he was so damned tall and subsequently pressed her lips against his own. She kissed him delicately at first, not to arouse but just to enjoy the simple touch. When her tongue swept out however, he captured it fiercely, allowing the muscle to tease and play and suddenly, she didn't want to *play*.

Need strummed up and down her body urgently, so breaking away from his mouth to press kisses against his jaw, upon his chin and along the tendons of his throat; she swept her tongue across the strong cords of flesh, giving a low mewl of hunger as her mouth trailed downwards to play with an erect nipple. Popping it into her mouth she sucked hard upon the little nub and smiled in pleasure as he hissed in surprise. Twirling it around the dimpled skin, she moved on to his other one, licking it gently she looked up at him with limpid eyes that conveyed the lust he'd born in her, she nipped at the nubbin aggressively.

Moving further down, she dropped kisses along the ridges of his eight pack, her breathing starting to come in pants as she neared his cock. It seemed bizarre to her that whilst she'd been intimate with the other two, that she really hadn't been with Dante. Feeling inordinately guilty about passing out from the surcease of pleasure the night before, she sank to her knees willingly and studied his dick for a second or two. Unsure of where to start and wanting more than anything to please him, she blew out a breath and fisted the base tight in her hands. Hearing his quick intake of breath steadied her nerves and with more eagerness than experience, she swirled her tongue around the glans of his cock, paying special attention to the lip that circled the head. Dragging her tongue over the slit, she pressed down into the small hole and then proceeded to slip her tongue along the vein that ran along the underside of his dick.

His taste was like nothing she'd ever experienced before, somehow musky but at the same time, in the most bizarre way, it felt like being in the woods, the fresh earthy scents surrounding her. Yet it was just Dante, that was how he smelled, fresh and clean but oh so masculine.

Flattening her tongue, she curved it around his dick, allowing the flexible muscle to touch as much as it possibly could. To trail along every inch of hard flesh.

When he growled, "Suck me, mate," his deep voice rumbled over her nerve-endings making her pussy clench hungrily. The combination of both order and endearment really packed a punch. She complied with his wishes by placing her open mouth, lips covering her teeth, around the head and flexing her mouth around him. Then gathering spit in her mouth, she proceeded to move her head up and down, grateful that she'd had the foresight to clench a hand around the base of his dick, when he started to thrust hungrily in her mouth. She let him, glad that he'd taken control of a situation where she'd been so uncertain of what to do.

When he clutched her head and pulled her away from him, she gave a whimper of disappointment, but on seeing his eyes flash with reciprocal need, she knew that it wasn't over. Dropping to the floor in front of her, he pulled her T-shirt over her head and lay it down behind her. Pushing her on to the covering, he looked at her with heavy-lidded eyes, his fingers moved over the cone of her breast, touching and teasing at the same time. Then they trailed down the center of her body and further on until they touched her intimately. His molten-gold gaze clashed with hers, and he grunted, "You enjoyed that, didn't you, mate? You're wet for me."

Whimpering slightly, she arched her back in an offering which he was quick to take. Obviously having changed his mind, he spun her around on to her hands and knees and within seconds, he plunged into her with a deep groan of relief.

She moaned at the depth of his plunges, at the new angle that touched different and sensitive nerves. When his fingers worked in league with his thrusts, she sobbed out helplessly, those clever wicked digits strummed their way around her clit, playing her as easily as they would a musical instrument. When the heel of his hand ground down suddenly on the small nubbin, she cried out hoarsely. When her arms became unable to support her weight, she crashed to the ground, but that just deepened his thrusts.

On a scream of pleasure, she felt the signals of a climax to end all climaxes. Like a tidal wave, it weighed her down, suffocating her in never-ending pleasure, blinding her to everything that wasn't Dante. With a final thrust, his cum splashed its way deep into her cunt and she felt herself being imprinted by him.

The thought that she would forever bear his mark was the final straw.   Her eyes fluttered shut to seek oblivion.

* * * *

"Please," she begged wearily, her voice hoarse from the constant plea that escaped her lips, her body throbbing as it demanded a completion that was being denied her.   Her position was shameless, Dante sat behind her and she lay against his chest and in between his legs.   Caden had reached for her thighs, spread them wide and hooked them over Dante's knees keeping them wide open, and simultaneously tilting her hips upwards and baring herself to their gaze. Dante had then grabbed her hands, intertwined their fingers and he'd raised her arms and hooked them behind his neck.

Caden's mouth had then proceeded to suckle at her pussy lips, his tongue alternately prodding her clit in a way that made her want to scream, then sweeping wildly along the length of her cunt and thrusting it inside her in a move that dragged her to the edge, right to the very edge only for him to drag her back inch by inch.

Her position arched her back and lifted her breasts for Shane's eager perusal, his mouth sucked at her erect nipples and would then bite and nip at them, leaving small bruises that would turn her on in the morning when she happened to look in the mirror.   His teeth raked the dimples on her nipples making her shudder. His touch combined with Caden's and the prod of Dante's cock in her lower back drove her insane.

When Caden moved completely away from her, she gave a scream of frustration which subsided when she noticed him grab their new best friend, the petroleum jelly.   Scooping a huge amount on to his fingers, he spread it copiously over her asshole, plunging his fingers deep inside her, lubricating her totally for their penetration.   She'd grown accustomed to the feel of her butt hole being played with, but it was something that always set her on edge, would always make her heart skip a beat and the breath falter in her chest. Perhaps that was normal, she only knew that when one of them was inside her there, it pushed her over the verge every time and now, after what felt like hours of being tortured, she longed for the drop with a desperate fervor.

Dante's hand slipped between them, his cock in hand, he rubbed the head along the rosette of her ass, pressing in a little, then pulling away. He did this so many times, that tears of frustration poured down her face and her body began to undulate against his. Whimpering in relief, when his dick finally pushed its way inside her, her body tensed, each limb taut, her back strung out in an overt display of her need.

Reacting more to the dipping of the bed than anything else, Emma's eyes popped open and she watched blearily as Shane settled himself over her lap and rested his butt on her stomach. His cock was greased and when he grabbed her breasts and molded them to his dick, she cried out in shock at such a contrast of feeling, her softness and his hardness. She arched her back a little more, opening her eyes and watching him with pleasurable as his cock worked its way through the tunnel of her breasts. Unable to help it, her eyelids fluttered at such an explicit shot and a shudder worked its way through her in reaction.

Her attention on Shane, she didn't notice Caden behind him about to work his cock inside her cunt. Feeling the blunt head prod her pussy, she cried out a little, she didn't think she would ever grow used to the feeling of such fullness, this was the third time they'd doubly penetrated her and it still felt as though her body couldn't accept them. As his cock forced its way inside her, she shuddered, her body quivering minutely. On feeling his hips jar against her own, Emma realized that they were in as deep as they could possibly go and the thought made her sight blacken dangerously. She was so close, it would take nothing to climax, to fall over into the precipice of pleasure that welcomed her each and every time she climaxed in their arms.

Working in a rhythm again, Dante rocked his hips alternating between Caden's thrusts so that they could both saw their cocks in and out of her. She couldn't help it when her body instinctively tightened around them, vice-like as though it was trying to force them out. But it did nothing of the sort, it turned them on, as little awareness of anything else as she had, even she could feel that. She wasn't the only one trembling now and, she thought with satisfaction, that it was about time they suffered like she did!

Unexpectedly, and more powerfully so because of it, Shane climaxed, his seed stringing along her chest and over her breasts. Feeling that warm seed coat her skin set her alight, it branded her, and she reveled in it. His jerky thrusts between her breasts continued, his grip on her tits growing harsher and harsher, but nevertheless jacking her need up and up. He seemed determined to milk every little drop from himself and as the glans of his cock accidentally brushed across her nipples, she cried out in shock as that little sensation suddenly erupted into a mass of volcanic proportions, engulfing her in feelings she couldn't cope with.

Everywhere they touched her, she could feel it keenly, feel Dante's chest hair abrade her back; felt the smoothness of Caden's skin as her thighs clutched at him, the veins on Shane's cock seemed to be imprinted on her flesh. The smallest touch became intense and so the feeling of their dual penetration exploded in her mind until with a long fraught scream, she climaxed in a burst of color.

* * * *

Could a person die from too much sex? Was it even possible?

For three days straight now, she'd been sharing a bed with Caden, Shane, and Dante, and while they tended to her somewhat sore areas in their own unique way, her body ached from the myriad of positions she'd been placed in. While she couldn't deny that she'd enjoyed every single second, she had noticed that her orgasms were lasting longer and longer, making her body so sensitive that Caden would trace a mole on her arm, play dot-to-dot along the expanse of skin, and she'd have to hold back the need to shudder, lust already brought to the fore. Going from 0 to 60mph in under one millisecond was starting to worry her. Sure it was fantastic to be so responsive, but *that* responsive? They were gorgeous and it was wonderful that they wanted her as badly as she wanted them, but wasn't it odd that the smallest touch rekindled the flame instantly?

It was actually rather frightening to go from such a sex-free life to this jam-packed sexual orgy. What frightened her even more was that she wouldn't change anything. Not even a minute of it. Did that mean she'd become a nymphomaniac? She was actually contemplating whether or not she had, because the thought of now living without sex made her stomach cramp and a tremor of fear quake through her system. She seriously didn't think she would be able to cope, she'd grown so used to them inside her in some position or other, she knew, just knew, that she'd suffer withdrawal pains!

Groaning at her unnecessary and useless introspection, she told herself to stop thinking. The rogue thoughts would resurface every now and then, though, and terrify her enough to want to jump one of them just to forget the hideous concerns flying around her mind, and then she'd wake up after an orgasm, usually one so powerful that the intensity had made her pass out and looking into their eyes, she would see their concern for her and her own doubts would quadruple. The scientist in her wouldn't let it rest, something was going on and she could only assume it was because they were Wolven. Something was happening to her, and, whatever it was, it wasn't getting any better. The more they touched her, the more she slept with them, the worse her symptoms became. She wasn't blind, for God's sake, she knew that something was going on inside her body, she just had absolutely no idea what it was!

Yesterday for example, the second day of the mating frenzy, she'd actually climaxed and had spent the following twenty minutes prone on the bed! She'd awoken in Dante's embrace, his arms tight around her and holding her close. She hadn't needed someone to tell her that he was worried about her, she hadn't needed to see the concern written on his face to know that. She'd lain sprawled across him, her head cushioned on his chest, her body comforted by the constant touch and somehow she'd slept comfortably, only awakening as she'd become aware that all their attention was focused on her. She'd sat up slightly, seen Caden and Shane laying beside Dante, leaning on their elbows to watch her, and had known that they'd been talking about her.

Being at the center of all their attention had at the very beginning caused a wave of self-consciousness to wash over her, but as the hours in their presence had passed, that had soon disappeared and had been exchanged for hearty enjoyment and relishing their appreciative looks. So finding herself at the center of their attention for a completely different reason, she'd huddled deeper into Dante's embrace, seeking comfort and receiving it, emptying her mind of whatever the hell it was that was happening to her.

Emma was no fool, something was happening to her, something that made her hyper-sensitive, made her suddenly aware of how they were feeling, made an orgasm push her into a faint . . . . It was something to do with their being Wolven and her being human. But, God help her, she didn't care. She wouldn't put a halt to their time together unless it was imperative and so far, the changes that were happening inside her, although worrying, she couldn't perceive as dangerous.

Standing in the shower stall, staring absentmindedly at her small bathroom, which was about the size of a postage stamp, she shook herself and turned on the faucet, drenching her hair in the water, she cleansed it with shampoo and conditioner. Dragging a sponge loaded with soap over her body, she fought the hyper-sensitivity that threatened to engulf her, had learned only yesterday how difficult washing could be, when she'd nearly passed out in the shower stall! Ignoring the tremors that shook her, she quickly cleaned herself and gave a shudder of relief when she could step out of the shower.

"Come in," she shouted out in response to the knock at the door, while she dabbed at her skin half-heartedly with a towel. She realized with a grimace that she was actually relieved that one of them would be there to help her back to the bedroom.

Shane popped his head around the door, the question he was about to ask falling dead on his lips as spying her standing there soaking wet a lascivious grin overtook his face and lust began to fill his gaze.

It astounded her at how quickly she could arouse them, and, watching his body move, the muscles work together, the long corded limbs play harmoniously, she couldn't help but stare as he strolled forward towards her. Easily lifting her up and perching her precariously on the sink, she had to spread her legs and clutch at him in order to not fall on the damn floor!

"Caden said to tell you that breakfast was ready," he said before growling, "but all I want to eat for breakfast, is you!" He lowered his head and nipped at the tendons of her neck.

She'd noticed that they did that often, biting the skin there until it was bruised and tender. In fact, she herself had started to do so to them! She tried to ignore it as yet another weird recollection over something that had occurred during these last few days, instead arching her neck, allowing him further access. She shivered weakly as her belly muscles undulated as his tongue curled around her earlobe. Jerking as he nipped it, she reached up to cup his face and dragged his mouth away from her shoulders and to her own. Eagerly attacking his mouth, she moaned against his lips as their tongues fought for domination.

Pressing herself against him, she shuddered as her sensitive skin was brushed against the soft hairs that covered his body.

When he pushed against her, their hips arched and his cock brushed her pussy. With a startled cry, her arms came around his neck in an effort to press herself ever closer to him. When a hand worked between them and he guided his cock into her needy cunt, a low urgent moan escaped her throat.

Clutching her to him, his hands cupping her ass, he lifted her away from the sink and walked away from the bathroom.

Eyes clenched tightly shut, her teeth bit at her lips as his walking jolted and jerked her instead of deeply thrusting his cock deep inside her. She felt a entirely different set of newly-discovered nerve-endings come to life. The stopping and starting seeming to pleasure and torment them both terribly. Grasping his shoulders tightly, she lowered her face into his neck. Unable to help herself, she bit deeply. It somehow seemed to help, to ease the lust that consumed her. Hearing his hiss of pleasure, she knew that he liked it. Her body undulated hungrily against him. It needed the thorough impalement of his cock, yet perversely enjoyed being teased in such a delicious manner.

Walking into her bedroom, he moved close to the bed. Settling awkwardly on the edge, he sat with his legs spread wide, which meant that her legs dangled and her feet didn't reach the floor. Laying back on the duvet, he crossed his arms under his head to support his neck and whispered throatily, "It's all yours, babe. Do what you want—take what you want."

Eyes a little blank, she tried to take stock of the position but found she was really unsure of what to do. Times like these her limited experience really became a hindrance! But rolling her hips a little, she realized that as she pulled away from him, her body weight would drag her down deeper on to his cock, and, with a startled whimper, she slowly worked her hips allowing his dick to rasp against the front wall of her pussy. The cords in her neck stood out prominently as pleasure worked its way throughout her system, her facial expression almost one of pain as those immense feelings worked through the lower part of her body.

Her breasts began to throb, needing to be touched, caressed, and she almost fell off Shane's lap in surprise when a pair of hands finally did cup her breasts, squeezing the nipples impossibly tight. She gave a keening moan and allowed herself to fall forward to lean against Shane's taut belly. Using the strength in her arms, she continued to thrust her hips and when those hands, Dante's, she'd recognize them in the dark, pinched at her nipples then abandoned them to wander down to her clit to pinch it with the same tenacity, she shattered into a million tiny pieces, her cunt fluttering and pulsing around Shane's cock without warning until, with a low grunt, his cum shot deep into her welcoming pussy.

The feel of that small burst in such a tightly cramped and packed area merely added to her pleasure, feeling so impaled, feeling him so gloriously deep, made a quake of sensation tremble along the surface of her skin, raising all the little hairs on her body until she was awash in a pool of awareness. Mentally she clung to Shane and Dante to survive the intensity of the battering, that wonderful awareness threatening to flood her senses so totally she didn't know if she'd survive.

Chapter Four

Staring at the ceiling, Dante alternated between nuzzling at Emma's jaw and inhaling her intoxicating scent. He'd been awake for a little while and had just relished being in his mate's presence. Awakening to her sprawled across him, her flesh touching every inch of his own had settled his wolf peacefully, and he realized that he'd never slept so well in all his life. She calmed and soothed the beast within him wonderfully and, for Dante, who had had to fight the beast for dominance since birth, it was fantastically freeing not to have to do so. Her presence had tamed his beast, and he would be forever grateful for it. Just a simple touch made his day. He knew that had he realized how vital a mate was to a Wolven, he would have started his search for her a long time ago. Instead, he'd been willing to allow destiny to run its course and, now that he knew how close his mate had been all along, he damned himself for not having found her sooner!

He wondered if the other two felt exactly the same, if so, then it could be because they were Alphas. Being Alpha meant that you had power and led your pack, but it also meant that that strength came from the inside, fighting your beast constantly and succeeding made you damned strong. Perhaps it was a characteristic all Alphas shared. Shrugging mentally, he inhaled deeply of her scent, allowed it to sink into his bones, into his very being.

It had changed over the last few days, the pheromone having disappeared entirely over the course of the first day. They'd then been blasted with pure undiluted Emma, which had driven them all fucking insane. On the second day, it had changed again, and all three of them had realized why. It was the reason why he was awake. Things were changing faster than he cared for, and they had to discuss it, needed to talk about the future and where they all stood. They'd left it too long already since none of them had been willing to face the possible outcome, happy instead just to be with their mate and enjoying the experience of awakening her sexually.

Feeling the other two stir awake, he turned his head towards Caden and looked pointedly at him. He jerked his head awkwardly and kicked Shane in the side. Obviously they understood what he'd wanted from them. As he watched, they rolled from the bed, their movements measured so as not to disturb Emma. He too moved gently, extricating his body as carefully as he could away from Emma's arms. Although there was nowhere on this Earth he would rather be, they had things to discuss and they couldn't be left any longer.

Moving away from the bed, their bare feet made little sound as they padded out of the bedroom, opening doors quietly until they were in the living room and free to make a little more noise. Shane lifted the cabin door out of the jamb. He'd managed to jam it in the other day and the only way to get in and out was to physically lift it away from the frame. Flinching at the slightest sounds they made, all three of them breathed a sigh of relief as they stepped outside into the woods. Jogging deeper into the forest, Dante sat down and leaned against a tree trunk, watching as Caden and Shane squatted down on the floor in front of him.

"Well?" he growled angrily. "What the fuck are we going to do?"

"There's nothing we can do. It's done," Caden answered pragmatically, a shrug of his shoulders indicating he wasn't all that worried.

"What do you mean, 'it's done'?" Dante asked, narrowed his eyes in anger. "We've been fucking our mate, who has yet to come to terms with what we are, and, to make matters worse, in the space of three days, one of us, we've no fucking idea who, has somehow managed to impregnate her."

"Dante, there's no need to lose your cool. It's done. There's nothing we can do but roll with the punches," Caden said, rolling his neck to the side, his aggression beginning to flare at Dante's continued anger.

"Roll with the fucking punches? Are you out of your god-damned mind? How the fuck can we? She has no idea that she's going to have to choose between us. Maybe she could be happy with the status quo, but, let's be realistic, it's more likely she'll choose. What happens if she doesn't choose the father, huh?"

Shane growled furiously.

Dante gave a saccharine smile. "That pisses you off, right? Thank you. For fuck's sake, Caden, we can't just let this rest. We have to discuss the possibilities here because something is bound to fuck up."

Caden jumped to his feet, pacing as he spoke, "Have you noticed this hyper-sensitivity of hers? I asked her yesterday if she was ordinarily so sensitive. She isn't. That's worrying me more than the fact that she might or might not choose the father. The fact that she passes out every fucking time she climaxes is worrying me, Dante. Forgive me for not thinking about myself and actually focusing on *my* mate, but one of us has to!" Dante hissed at him.

Caden jerked his chin out threateningly. "Come on, fuck-wit, fight me. Show you don't give a shit about that woman, just about your own fucking needs! Something is going on with her, and I'm worried. Aren't you two worried?"

Shane answered for Dante, "Of course, we're worried. But, as you said earlier, there's nothing we can do. She's obviously reacting to fucking three Wolven."

"That doesn't make it alright, Shane! What the fuck is going on with you two? I, for one, am concerned. Sure, it strokes my ego that *my* mate climaxes and is dead to the world for the next twenty minutes, but it's not normal. What happens if it affects the pups?"

Dante blew a breath out noisily. "She's probably just reacting to our DNA, Caden. If she is meant to be all three of ours mates, then her body will be able to handle it. Don't forget her body is being bombarded by three Alpha's DNA a couple of times a day. I'm not surprised she has some reactions to it. It's only natural."

"I don't care if it's natural, Dante. It doesn't make it right. I think we need to take her to a healer or something, just to make sure everything is alright. She can't fucking shower without almost passing out, you think that's natural? I watched her the other day, she can't even pass the sponge over her body without shuddering!" Caden shook his head angrily. "You're not looking at the bigger picture, which is her welfare. What's the point in fighting over whose mate she is if she doesn't survive fucking pregnancy, huh? Stop thinking with your cocks. This whole problem goes away if she dies, for fuck's sake! Do you want to be without her?" He smiled derisively at their flashing shifting eyes. "No, I didn't think so. We have to care for her more than we have to care for ourselves, otherwise we don't get her. If she doesn't survive having one of our pups, we lose her forever!"

Shane spoke up, concern evident in his voice, "Maybe it's just the fact that she's pregnant. There was bound to be some reaction to having Wolven pups, even if they're half-blood. Caden, I understand where you're coming from, alright?" he said soothingly, "but like Dante said, the Fates chose her, they wouldn't have picked her if her body wasn't capable of having Wolven mates and pups. All three of us are concerned about her, but I can also understand Dante's point. There's a real possibility that she won't choose the father, and, personally, although you two are my best friends and are like my brothers, I don't want you raising *my* pup. I want to be there. So where does that leave us? Are we going to have to take her choice out of the equation and just demand that she stays with the pup's father? Or are we just going to hope for the best and hope that she chooses the father? I, for one, am not happy just to let this happen without any of my input. I want to plan this out." He cracked his knuckles aggressively. Just thinking about having no control in this situation put him on edge.

"Neither of you have even considered that these changes to her body might mean something else. She could be having more than one pup to different fathers," Dante said, issuing a nasty laugh as he saw the idea sweep over the other two men. "The Fates really would be fucking with us then, wouldn't they? Already they've messed with our lives, one mate between three Alphas! Now, can you imagine, two pups, two different fathers. That will really freak our *human* mate out, and that's just what we need. And how the hell are we even going to tell her what's happening? She's a scientist, she's noticed the changes. I can see her looking at us, expecting an answer . . . . How are we going to handle this?"

"I don't know, Dante, I really don't, but we're going to have to do something. I mean now that she's pregnant, I'm not happy with her being here in this cabin. I need to get back to my pack, as do you two. I don't want anyone guarding her but me or you two. How are we even going to deal with the logistics? It blows my fucking mind," Shane muttered angrily.

"I hesitate to say it, without either of you two biting off my head, but there's nothing we can do. I don't want her to have no say in her future. She's an independent woman. She's relied on no man for the last twenty-nine years of her life, she won't be happy having every aspect of her life controlled. While she's pregnant, and until we know who the father or fathers are, it looks like we're going to have to merge the packs."

A moment's silence filled the circle. Dante tilted his head to the side, his eyes glaring angrily at Caden,

"Are you out of your goddamn mind? Merge the packs? Merge the fucking packs? Break with tradition? Break with every Alpha instinct and rule as a trio? Are you fucking insane?"

Caden stood his ground, his stance becoming aggressive in the face of such insolence. "For *my* mate, I'll do what's necessary to not only protect her but to keep her happy. I hope the pups are mine, and she doesn't have to be mated to you two dicks, because it sounds like she'd have a shit life with you by her side! Don't you even care about the changes that are about to take place in her life? Don't you give a shit?

"She's supposed to be your mate. A Wolven's life changes to protect and ensure his mate's life is a happy one. Seems like neither of you two are willing to make that many changes to your so-called happy existence. I'll be pleased to take her off your hands, you fuckers," Caden answered sweetly, watching in pleasure as Dante stood slowly and Shane rolled to his feet. They deserved this, the bastards, what did they think Emma was? What century did they think they were in? It was the twenty-first and as much as he longed to grab her and drag her back to his pack lands, for his life to merrily go on as normal as hers was dragged into uproar, he couldn't do it to her, wouldn't do it to her, and he refused to allow it to happen.

Clenching his fists, he allowed the two to walk closer to him. If fighting them stopped them from being so fucking selfish, then fight them he would. Emma was more than worth it. He studied Shane for a second, knew he'd be the first one to make a move. He'd always been the more impatient of the three. He studied Shane's side for a second, waiting for a glimpse of tensed muscles to show him which arm he was going to attack with. Seeing a small play of tension, he immediately ducked, missing the outstretched arm by a hair's breadth and flung out a tautened arm out to pummel Shane's stomach. He caught Shane straight in the gut and watched with a smile as he shrank back and clutched at his stomach, "Come on, fight for her, you bastards! Or isn't she worth it? Come on, Dante," he said, flexing his fingers in a bring-it-on motion, watching as his sally easily riled the other man.

The two men studied each other warily, each waiting on feet ready to spring them into action. His attention on Dante, Caden only just managed to miss the punch that Shane aimed his way. He jumped back, but it didn't stop the punch from jumping way off target and landing against his nose, glancing just off his cheekbone. "Bastard," he hissed as blood flowed freely from his obviously broken noise. He watched in pleasure as Shane clenched his jaw and studied his closed hand, flexing it softly. He grinned, thankful that his broken appendage had at least caused Shane's fist some damage.

Holding his forearm against his nose stopped the blood flow somewhat, but not enough and rather than waste time waiting for Dante to move, because he was a tactical fucker, would wait a long time just to settle upon a weakness and to follow through with an attack and Shane had just handed him one on a plate, Caden rushed forward and cried out triumphantly as, on his first blow, he managed to kick Dante's legs from under him, kicking against the other man's ankle in a stab-like movement that placed a hell of a lot of pressure on the joint. Surprised that Dante went down so easily, he jumped out of the way and grunted angrily as Dante's hand flung out and grabbed him by the calf, dragging him to the floor in a not so dissimilar move. He landed with a thump but immediately scrambled out of the way because he knew that Shane would be waiting to pounce and that he had to be on his feet to take the hit.

Even through the shudder of his body, as it realigned itself after a nasty fall, he couldn't help but grin at how equal they really were, but then they were Alphas, had to fight dirty and be nasty bastards sometimes just to stay on top. "Come on, Shane, break my fucking arm, you know you want to," he taunted. "How dare I suggest that you wouldn't care for your mate?" he jeered. "I'll tell you how, she's not a fucking suitcase, pleased to be dragged around the state, and if you two even consider treating her like that, then you don't deserve her at all." He jumped on his toes and brought his fists up to his chest in a classic boxing stance. He managed to dance his way nearer to Shane and got in a few successful jabs. Shane's hand sliced through the air and thudded against his already weakened side. With a groan of pain, Caden shrank back and waited for another attack from Dante.

"There's no point to this fight," Dante murmured quietly, sitting cross-legged and patiently, his aggression having obviously dissipated. "We've already ascertained that none of us will ever win a fight and that if one of us does, then it will be by chance or injury, and, when the battle is this important, I'm not willing to lose out because you bastards know where a damned Beta once managed to hurt me. Caden you've got a broken nose, I think you've sprained my ankle, and undoubtedly Shane has some sort of internal injury from your punch to the gut," He said a little sarcastically, "Has Emma's honor been restored yet? Can we get back to the matter at hand?"

"I don't know. Have you stopped thinking with your cocks and awoken to the fact that she could be in danger by bearing our children?" Caden reproached derisively.

"Son of a bitch," Shane hissed, "we were never unconcerned when it came to her, Caden. Of course we give a damn, even if it wasn't written into our genetic code to care for our mates, you fuck-wit."

"Don't start him up again, Shane," Dante warned. "Look, Caden you're right, we obviously need to look into why she's passing out so frequently and why all of a sudden she's so hyper-sensitive, but I guarantee that it will be something to do with her being pregnant. That's why, if I haven't shown any, I'm not concerned.

Of course, I wish it wasn't the case, I wish that she reacted to bearing our pups as she would if we were human, but as soon as I scented that we'd impregnated her, I expected these sort of complications. If you really think about it, I'm sure you too realized that a human wouldn't bear Wolven offspring without some sort of mishap or slight complication!

"Because I focused on a different matter than your did doesn't mean I care for her or her welfare any less than you do. As Shane said, it's written in our DNA that we cherish our mates. You were out of order to even suggest that by not discussing her pregnancy and its side-effects we were somehow lacking as mates. It's very important that we discuss the future because I'm concerned about that. Pregnancy issues can be dealt with as and when throughout the duration, but losing my mate to one of you two, perhaps losing my pup to one of your packs, doesn't rest well with me. You suggested we merge packs. I admit I didn't react well to that, but if it's at all a possibility, then we'll just have to deal with it as it comes. If it means that we each have our mate, then I'm sure we'll deal with the consequences accordingly and any discord in our packs will be handled. As you say, we don't want Emma to be unhappy, and, if our packs are unhappy by this move, then as Alpha female, she's bound to bear the brunt of it. I certainly don't want that!

"I think we're going to have to discuss this with her and see what she thinks," he said, sighing noisily. "If she believed that this was just a few days of hot sex, then she needs to come to terms with what we are to her. She's also going to have to deal with being pregnant. I know you don't want to take her choices away from her, Caden, but have you ever thought that maybe the Fates chose her for us and us for her? Maybe she needs all three of us to complete her? Because her society sees a ménage relationship as distasteful, she could completely rule it out and not consider being with us in that kind of family unit.

Maybe we need to present her with a *fait accompli,* that way, we all win!"

"I don't like taking her choices away either, but I think you're right, Dante. If she reacts to the early stages of pregnancy the way she has, then how is she going to cope with the later stages? She's going to need us all. Maybe it was fated this way purposely. We're all Alphas, we're all busy men, this way one of us will always be there for her while the other two deal with pack business. I think we need to stop thinking about her choosing one of us. I think we're going to have to present ourselves to her *as is.* It will be best for all of us, and we'll make her happy. She won't be living in a human environment anyway, she'll be in pack lands, so there's no concern about any disapproval by society if that is one of her arguments." Shane sighed before he continued. "If we do it this way, we don't have to worry about the pups not being raised by their fathers."

"You're both right. We're going to have to discuss this with her more in-depth, explain things to her so that she doesn't think we're fucking with her head, but as well, I think it's wise to present the unit as a foursome," Caden conceded. "I suppose it also makes sense that we get this out of the way as soon as possible. If she's showing signs of pregnancy so early on, she needs to be aware of the whys. Emma's no idiot. It might annoy her that she's pregnant, but at least she'll be aware of why these things are suddenly happening to her, why her body is changing. If she knows the source of the changes, then she's less likely to worry. I've noticed the little glances as well, Dante, like she's asking me what the hell is going on. I think she deserves to know and as soon as possible."

"Well, we're all agreed then," Dante answered sarcastically and rolled to his feet easily. He walked over to Caden, slapped him on the shoulder, and did the same to Shane. They began the walk back to the cabin slowly and unhurriedly, all of them thankful that peace had been restored within the group.

"She's probably still asleep," Shane said, rubbing at his bruised fist while he walked.

"Hopefully, she is. The more rest she gets, the better. I would say it might be wise to not sleep with her anymore, but I don't think that would be of any help. Every time we fuck her, she's getting used to the Wolven DNA. Being pregnant with non-human DNA multiplying inside her, her body could react to the child as an intruder. If we bombard her with our own, then I imagine that will stop it from happening and the baby will be alright. You're right, Caden, we need to go to a healer, someone who knows what the fuck is happening and why it's happening. I don't want her tiring because we're keeping her up all the time, but if it's important she grow accustomed to our genetic code, then we'll just have to force ourselves to fuck her," Dante joked and grinned as the other two laughed easily.

With a perplexed frown on his face displacing the grin, Shane's head tilted to the side, "Guys, the door's open."

"We replaced it, didn't we?" Caden asked hurriedly, starting to sprint to the cabin.

"Yeah, you don't think someone scented the pheromone?"

"That wore off days ago. Anyway, she's loaded with our scent now," Dante said, frowning. "Emma must have lifted it out. Why would she do that?"

"You don't think she's gone somewhere?" Shane asked uneasily.

"Why would she go somewhere?" Caden said, confusion evident in his tone. "She works at the cabin. Her life is there. There's no need for her to go out."

"Maybe she has run away?" Shane replied hesitantly.

"Why the hell would she do that?" Caden asked.

"How the fuck should I know? But it's a possibility! She could be freaked out by what's happening to her," Shane answered as they reached the door and ran into the small cabin. Immediately heading to the bedroom, they saw that the bed was unmade and her closet door was wide open. A few items of clothing trailed on the floor, indicating she'd packed in a hurry.

"Fuck, where the hell could she have gone to?"

"We'll have to trace her as Wolven, her scent will be stronger. She can't have managed to go that far. We've only been gone about forty-five minutes!" Dante muttered and then said quickly, "Come on, we'd best find her."

All three men transformed and ran off into the woods, their noses close to the ground in search of their mate's scent.

* * * *

With a hidden smile, Emma allowed Dante to disentangle his arms from her own, she felt like undulating against the bed in pleasure, felt like the proverbial cat who had got all the cream. It was amazing how within the space of three days, she'd grown so accustomed to laying atop one of the men and embracing them throughout the night, their limbs intertwining as the hours passed. It must have pleased them as well because they had not only made no complaints, they'd each taken it in turn to be her mattress. She assumed that it resolved the issue of where they all slept. With her in the center, albeit astride one of them, they easily lay beside her. She'd noticed that they never touched sexually and she assumed that it was obviously a no go area. She wasn't bothered by that at all though, she'd had her eyes opened enough these last few days, she didn't need to be enlightened any further! But her sleeping in the position she did meant they could join her on the bed and not feel uncomfortable sleeping next to another guy and she had to admit that she liked sleeping in such cramped quarters. It was wonderful awakening in their presence, knowing they were close at hand and all she had to do was reach out and she'd feel their flesh against her own. Holding back a sigh of wonder, she kept her eyes firmly shut and pretended to carry on sleeping. She tried to keep her lips from twitching into a smile as they all tried to make as little noise as possible to ensure she continued sleeping. She didn't know why she didn't tell them she'd woken up, she just lay there silently, waiting to see what they were going to do.

As they stepped away from the bed and walked out of the room, she frowned a little, as it was the first time they'd left her completely alone for the past three days. Unless she was in the bathroom, one of them was with her at all times. Shuddering a little as the cotton sheets rasped against her skin, she gave a groan of annoyance as that damned hyper-sensitivity reared its ugly head again. Sleeping against one of the men seemed to help it a little, as though the constant pressure of skin against skin eased it somewhat. Raising herself on to her knees, she quickly jumped off the bed and walked to the door, ready to go and see what they were doing. But on her way, she heard the unmistakable sound of the front door being moved away from the frame and with a scowl she quickly walked over to the curtains and watched as Dante, Shane, and Caden walked out the door and began to run into the woods, their pace quickening as they ran from her house and deeper into the trees.

Clapping a hand to her mouth as her eyes widened in shock at the sight of them running away from the cabin, she took a few steps backwards, her movements awkward and jerky, staggering as she made her way back towards the bed. A fine quivering tremble overtook her limbs as her mind collated the evidence and came to the only possible conclusion-they were leaving her. It had been the pheromone that had attracted them to her after all and now it had worn off, they were going, abandoning her. They were leaving her without even a goodbye. Unable to help herself, sobs began to rack her small frame, tears poured copious paths over the curves of her cheeks as she contemplated a future without them and realized that she couldn't.

An animal-like sound of grief roared around the room as she came to terms with the fact that she wasn't their mate, that it had been the pheromone, that the scientist had been correct all along. Huddling on the bed, she pressed her face into the pillow and retreated slowly away from it as she realized that their scent covered the bed linen. Everything smelled like them. She stood up and walked away from the bed, her eyes glued to it all the while, the place where she'd found so much happiness, where she'd finally felt as though she belonged. Pressing a hand to her trembling mouth, Emma backed herself against a wall and slowly slid down to the floor. Looking around the wrecked room, where she'd finally been at peace with herself and the world at large, it seemed incredible how within the space of five minutes, the last three days came tumbling, crumbling, crashing down around her head.

She wanted to damn herself, scream in rage at allowing them to get so close when she'd always known that there had been a possibility it was the pheromone they were attracted to. She'd always known that, but she'd also wanted to experience what they offered and God, she had, and now, thinking about never experiencing them again, felt like a knife wound to the chest. Watching them run into the woods had to be the most horrific moment in her life, seeing them walk away from her, without even a goodbye, it tore a bleeding gash down the very center of her heart. How could they just leave her? Didn't she deserve a farewell? Why allow her to believe that she was their mate then just abandon her when they realized otherwise?

Teardrops continued to fall from her eyes. She sat limply on the floor, staring unseeingly at the bed. On a sob of pure grief, she scrambled determinedly to her feet. She couldn't stay here, couldn't stand to be at the cabin that she'd shared with them. The pheromone obviously worked. She could go to the university, take her notes on the new molecular structure of the pheromone, and stay with a colleague, stay in a hotel, anywhere. She just couldn't stay here.

Rushing to the closet, she dragged a pair of jeans and a T-shirt on and grabbed some other items from hangers and into a case that she stored on the top shelf of the small closet. She didn't care that she was leaving a mess, that she was leaving her home vulnerable to intruders with a damaged front door. She just had to escape. In three days, it seemed as though they'd imprinted themselves into her memory. Just looking around the bedroom, she could see them there. She wouldn't be able to cope with 'seeing' them in the kitchen and living room as well! Looking at places where they'd made love to her, where they had taken her to heaven and back down to Earth. She just couldn't cope with it.

Grabbing the half-zipped case, she rushed out of the bedroom and into her lab, reached for her notes and the remaining liquid in the fridge so she'd have some excuse to salvage her pride when she turned up at the university unexpectedly. She could lie and say that the tears that wouldn't stop were ones of happiness, relieved as she was to have a working pheromone that had passed the first stage of trial.

Shoving everything into a plastic bag, she hurried to the front door and kicked at it when the damned thing wouldn't open. Moving it slightly, she realized that lifting it opened it a little and with a strength she didn't know she possessed, she somehow managed to lift the heavy door open. Rushing outside, she walked around the house to where her car was currently parked, its space having been taken up by the wolf's cage. Quickly pushing the case into the back seat and dropping the bag on to the front seat, she jumped in and started the engine, eager to escape the cabin that had once been her haven and had now become her hell.

It didn't take long for her to exit the woods, her car

quickly eating up the miles on the road that led to the highway. Emma knew it was dangerous to drive in her state, but she wanted to escape the forest, needed to retreat from the memories of these past few days.

On the very cusp of joining the highway, she pulled over to the side of the road and lifted her shirt up to dry her eyes. With her blurry vision she really shouldn't have been driving. She knew it was irresponsible, but she'd just had to get away, and, with a teary exhausted sigh, she rested her head against the steering wheel. Her body felt as though she'd been in a car crash, everywhere ached, but then that's what happened when you had your heart broken by unthinking, unfeeling bastards, she supposed, continuing to sob.

She partially blamed herself for having gotten so caught up in the situation, to have actually told herself that if they left her, it wouldn't matter because at least she'd experienced real emotion! How could she have been so lax with her own heart? How could she have let them break down her defenses so easily? She didn't know, all she could say was that being with them had felt so right, so natural that, had she not seen them run away with her own two eyes, she would never have believed it.

Perhaps Wolven did this. Perhaps they fucked women and just left them heartbroken. Because she'd fallen in love with them, no matter how impossible it had seemed, she had, they'd broken down the walls surrounding her heart and were firmly lodged there, and she knew they would be for a long time. "Dammit!" she screamed and slapped her hands against the steering wheel. In a frenzy of rage, she smacked and slapped it, screaming her hurt out and releasing the venomous pain that seemed to wear its way through her skin until visible wounds scored her flesh. When the fury abated, she ignored her sore hands and settled herself against the wheel on a flurry of sobs. So deep in her distress was she, that she didn't hear or feel the door opening, only felt the hand cover her arm. She jerked back with a shriek of shock.

With bleary eyes, she looked into Caden's beloved face and shrank back from him. "What are you doing here?" she asked dazedly. "You left!" she said accusingly.

"We didn't!" he defended himself. "You did!"

"You didn't even say goodbye," she cried out sadly.

"That's because we weren't leaving. We were going for a run," he replied earnestly, rubbing at his nose as he answered.

Narrowing her eyes, she caught the slight hesitation before he commented on their leaving and the unusual gesture. She muttered accusingly, "You're lying! What the hell is wrong with your nose?"

He sighed wearily. "Emma, my mate, I've just had to run from your cabin to here to come and get you. Can we please talk about this back at the cabin? There's nothing wrong with my nose, and, if you'll just move over, I can drive us home, okay?"

"Can you drive?" she asked with a frown. Surely Wolven didn't learn how to drive, did they?

He looked affronted. "Of course I can drive! Do you think I would put you in danger by suggesting I drive us when I was a complete novice behind the wheel?"

"Sorry," she replied, feeling a little small at his affront. She hadn't meant to insult him, but it seemed as though she had. Climbing out of the door, she followed him around to the other side where he opened the door for her and waited for her to seat herself before closing it. She mumbled her thanks as he sat down but otherwise sat quietly, saying little as he started the engine and drove them home. She watched him and frowned in confusion. Why had he lied? Maybe she'd been wrong. They hadn't left her. They'd just gone for a run or something into the forest. But why had he lied about their reasons for entering the woods. She knew he'd lied, she'd been able to tell from his hesitation. It seemed so bizarre that for three days straight they hadn't left her knowingly alone. In fact, as soon as she awoke within five minutes they were beside her. That was if she managed to wake up without disturbing them at all! Even when she showered, or used the bathroom, if she was too long, they asked her if she was alright. It seemed so strange that all three of them would leave her and so abruptly.

"I can see you over there thinking. Stop it, mate. You're wrong. We weren't leaving you, that I can promise you!" His gaze switched from watching the road to capture her gaze for a moment.

It confirmed to her that she'd been wrong, and, even though she felt like a fool, she knew there was something going on for them to have left her in the first place!

She looked away and whispered, "Even though you're here, I feel like my heart is breaking."

She heard the hiss of his breath before he pulled the car to a standstill, reached for her, and whispered, "Your heart need never break, mate, whenever you're with me, Dante, or Shane. Know that your heart is in safe hands!"

Clinging to him for a second, she said, "I can't stop crying. I don't understand why I'm so emotional!"

He hesitated for a second, she knew, just knew, that he understood why she was such an emotional wreck, but he didn't answer her, just hugged her close and whispered in that foreign language that she didn't understand and that they only spoke in when they thought she was asleep, "*Ya palyubil tebya s pervava vzglyada.*"

"What does that mean?"

His only reply was to tap his nose secretively, but he smiled at her and leaned down to press a soft kiss to her lips.

She responded to his gentleness and opened her mouth to touch her tongue to his. His presence soothed her soul and calmed her battered heart. But the feeling that she'd lost them hadn't eased any even though his arms surrounded her. She felt as though she was playing a waiting game, felt as though she would forever be waiting for them to leave her because she'd been stupid enough to open herself to the pain by accepting them into her life.

Maybe that was what love was though. By opening herself up to it, she'd opened herself up to hurt, and, although she didn't like the vulnerability and promised herself that she would try to separate herself from them a little, she knew that she wouldn't be able to manage it. She needed them, now, needed them badly. It wasn't just her heart that cried out for them, her body was the main offender. Being with him, tongues tangling easily, soothingly, his lips pressed against hers, she felt at peace, her body felt at peace. She felt right in a way that she'd never been before.

When he disentangled their tongues and pressed a little kiss to her mouth, he smiled as she kissed him back, then pulled away to start the short drive back to the cabin. Although she couldn't deny that she felt better seeing him, she felt more reassured as driving up to her home the other two men were there waiting impatiently for the car to stop.

As soon as it did, Dante dragged the door open and hauled her into his arms. He muttered into her hair, "Where the hell did you go?"

"She thought we'd left her," Caden answered for her, his tone dry as he watched Dante clutch her close.

"Why the hell did she think that?" he asked angrily.

"Hey, I am here you know!" she grumbled and pulled herself out of his arms even though it was where she longed to be. She stepped away from him only to be swooped into Shane's embrace. Unable to help it, she clung to him and closed her eyes at his scent, at his touch. Blowing out a pent up breath, she said, "You were running into the forest. What the hell was I supposed to think?"

Dante frowned but noted Caden's flashing glance. "I don't know what you were supposed to think, but you shouldn't have thought we were leaving you ,and you shouldn't have run away! You're our mate, Emma. I told you that! Do you think we would just abandon our mate?"

She wisely didn't answer but closed her mouth stubbornly and pressed herself into Shane's arms, allowing him to comfort her.

"Do you think I could leave you?" he murmured quietly, for her ears only.

She shook her head into his shoulders and, despite herself, even though it made her want to scream in frustration, tears started to flood her eyes.

Feeling the wetness on his shoulder, he mouthed to the other two, "She's crying." Sweeping a hand up and down her back to comfort her, he whispered, "It's alright, mate, don't worry, you weren't to know."

"It was the first time all three of you had left me. I didn't know what to think," she said testily, then pulled away. "Why am I so god damned emotional and sensitive? I hate it. I hate this. Why do I feel like this?" she said before yelling, "I don't cry, I never cry, and all I've done this morning is cry! It's all your fault," she said accusingly before breaking away and running into the cabin through the still-open front door. She ran straight to her bedroom and slammed the door closed before she flung herself on to the bed and proceeded to . . . cry!

Chapter Five

So the bastards had found a mate, had they? Smirking in contemplation, Kyle found himself holding back a laugh as he took malicious pleasure in discovering that three Alphas from some of the most influential packs in the US had a weakness. And he was one of the very first to know about it. Probably the only one to know about it.

With an internal chuckle, Kyle leaned back against a tree trunk and decided that although for the first part of his life the Fates had fucked with his existence, they had more than made up for it by giving him this little piece of knowledge. This little tidbit of information would be the cause of many a problem in the Wolven world for the unforeseeable future, and he looked forward to being at the very center of that anarchy. Unable to stop the grin from overtaking his face at the thought of such disruption, Kyle just barely managed to control the urge to laugh out loud. Clasping his hands together to stop himself, he hung them loosely over his knees as he continued to listen with relish to the other men's conversation.

Unable to believe it, his eyes glistened merrily as he realized they'd actually managed to impregnate her so soon and that they had no idea which man was the father. Priceless, he thought nastily, exalting in his good fortune. It seemed incredible that he now had two of their weaknesses within the palm of his hand, and, he was sure as hell going to exploit them, and he was going to enjoy doing it! The bastards deserved it and so did their packs. They may have forgotten him, but with him they weren't so lucky. As far as he was concerned they were still filed in the 'Not yet dealt with' compartment of his brain. Now he finally had a chance to change all that. There was no way he was going to allow them to get away with the shit they'd dealt upon his head. He deserved to get his revenge, and he was going to get it. Come hell or high water, he would be avenged, and it was only a matter of time before they felt the pain of that vengeance.

He'd scented the bitch, their mate, earlier in the week. The scent had been strong but so had the natural wolf's, neither had overly appealed to him, but since he considered this his territory he'd investigated further. He'd padded along to see where the hell it was coming from and had discovered amongst the flurry of wolves surrounding the caged wolf, his three enemies. Watching them closely, he'd noticed that the three men had charged after the unknown woman. Intrigued, he'd hung around the woods in wait for their next move. He didn't know what had intrigued him overly. Sure it was more than unusual for three Wolven to approach a human female in their shifted forms, but there could have been a number of reasons for why that had happened. What had made him stay and see what the hell was going on, he really didn't know, but he was sure damn glad that something had, because now he had the power to break them and that power felt really fucking good.

It felt even better knowing that they had no idea what was around the corner. He was determined to make it as hellish as possible for them. Why shouldn't he? They'd made his life unbearable. It was only because he was a resilient bastard that he'd managed to survive at all, no thanks to their packs and the three schmucks behind him, who were now whining about their mate. He wanted to crow at the irony, but he withheld it for another time.

No, he shrugged his shoulders nonchalantly, he'd go ahead with the plan that was forming in his head because they deserved it, deserved to be punished, and it seemed as though he were the only one with big enough balls to do it. Well, do it he would, and he'd enjoy every damned second of it.

Over the course of his life, he'd discovered that Wolven worked in two ways. The first rule governing their life was that the pack was everything. They grew up learning about their pack's history and then they were taught how to protect its future, its past, and its present. Their lives revolved around their extended 'family' and, as a rule, all children were protected by the adults until maturity. Humans were both feared and respected for what they could do, for the power they held. But all children were taught to leave them primarily alone and secondly to dislike them on the principle that any knowledge they held of or about the Wolven would destroy their species, would decimate them as a nation. Their pack mentality changed after reaching maturity, their priority changing to encompass the discovery of their mate and the whole cycle started again, with any children the two mates had having the pack as the focal point to their existence.

Kyle hadn't been lucky enough to be raised in such an idyllic way, had had no protection from anyone, had in fact been left to fend for himself. The unfortunate bastard offspring of a slut who'd fucked a Wolven and had been unlucky enough to beget him a son. She'd been saddled with a kid and she'd let Kyle know that he was the thorn in her side from day one. He'd become accustomed to being treated like shit by his mother. As a fourteen year old, being practically beaten to death by one of his darling mother's latest conquests, had been the last straw. He'd left his mother and the only home he'd ever known and gone in search of his father. He hadn't gone with stars in his eyes, just with a relentless burning need to know and learn more about whatever the fuck he was. A year before his exploration, he'd realized what his body could do, that he could actually change into a wolf, having discovered it quite by chance after being slapped by his mother. He'd never reacted well to being abused by her, but until his teenage years had had no real means of defending himself. On that particular day he'd managed to run away, had sought out his room as a place of solace, and with the excess emotion coursing through his veins, hate a burning flame in his heart, he'd shifted into something he'd only read about in horror stories and action movies.

During that year of living rough, he'd never managed to find his other parent, but he had come across other packs, the first of which being Dante's. Fully expecting to be welcomed into the pack's bosom, a lost child that should be greeted as such and would be cared for and educated until he'd reached maturity, he'd instead been shunned almost instantly. Shocked, he'd moved on, the subsequent packs he'd found, Shane's and Caden's, had treated him equally, casting him out before he'd even had a chance to settle. He had realized then that if he wanted to survive he'd have to rely on himself just as he always had. And he'd managed to do just that.

Just thinking about it now, four years on, had the power to sour his mood within an instant and piss him off so utterly that a blind rage could bury him. He'd overcome his past, no thanks to them, had even managed to create his own pack of lone wolves, who like him hadn't been welcomed by the established packs and had had to fend for themselves. He'd even managed to stay as the Alpha, which at the age of nineteen was pretty shocking. He'd come across wolves double his age who had challenged him for leadership and had managed to vanquish each and every one of them. He was strong, maybe that was because of his past. Always a festering wound, it gave him the strength and cruelty to fight without compassion and beat men who were probably more appropriate as Alpha. He'd clung to his seat of power, and he was damned proud of that feat. What he'd never managed to do however, was overcome the scorn that he'd been greeted with, had never been able to overcome the injustice of it all.

What Kyle needed was closure. It was time to forget the past, to get on with the present and enjoy the future, but until he could avenge the spirit of that boy, he knew that he would never be able to rest. Just thinking about that young boy, who'd been so naïve in hoping to be accepted by what he'd once considered brethren, made an intense and overwhelming anger reverberate through his system, his heart pounding a furious tattoo as he recalled his lost innocence. With a scornful smile, he knew that it was time to expunge all that rage, and revenge was the best method.

Until now, he'd pretty much steered clear of the three Alphas, content with what he had and pleased to lead his small pack of rogue wolves. Fully aware that he had no real power in the Wolven world and that he hadn't a cat in hell's chance of actually managing to hurt either them and their packs. Then he'd scented the three Alphas in woods he considered his territory and had followed them to see what they were up to. Now it seemed as though the festering wound would be lanced, and he knew a perfect way to do it and in a way that would cause maximum devastation. It all depended on the woman. Their mate.

He'd seen her the other day. She was a little scrawny but attractive enough to fuck. But he'd been more interested in the men's reaction to her than his own thoughts. At first he'd believed the scent she'd been exuding was the cause for their frenzy. Wolven were taught to despise humans and ignore them as much as possible, one of the main reasons he'd been shunned- but now, three days on, he was eavesdropping on their argument and he had the real reason why they'd been mad for her. She was their mate. He couldn't believe his luck.

There was no point in challenging the Alphas, he was strong but not strong enough to take on and beat all three of them, even single-handedly it would be difficult in their prime and mature as they were, and although they led the packs that had cast him out, he was intelligent enough to realize that it was the pack who had spoken, who had refused to welcome a half-blood from a non-mated coupling and who had been raised by the humans they were taught to despise. That didn't take the pain of their prejudice away and he thought both the Alphas and their packs deserved to be punished for such small-mindedness. It was the reason that, even if he could win, a challenge wouldn't be enough.

He was the product of his surroundings. They could have reformed him, changed his life for the better, yet they'd chosen not to. Had chosen to expel him from their bosom and leave him to fend for himself. They had had no compassion for him, a young teenage boy, so why should he show any for them? He was shrewd enough to realize that the plan he was formulating in his head, however, would hurt all three men *and* all three packs. By pushing ahead with his scheme, he was jeopardizing the future of each pack, and, with a pleased smile, he knew that it would have far-reaching long-term effects.

If his memory served him right, she was good enough to fuck, so the basic ingredients to his plan were to abduct her and take her deep into the heart of his pack lands. There he'd fuck her, see what she was like in the sack. If she made it worth his while, he wouldn't kill her, he'd let her live, but either way, if she lived or died, she would bear a child and he would raise it. As simple and cunning as that. But so effective. He, the rogue not fit to clean the shit on their shoes, would be raising the Alphas' child as his own. Oh the irony, he thought with menace.

Kyle knew his plan would work to full effect when he heard them talk about merging the packs. An Alpha's son usually took over a pack after the father became too frail to lead or died. He would have to prove his mettle, but a child born to an Alpha and his soul mate was almost always a legitimate heir to the leadership.

By taking their mate and their unborn child, he would take away their packs' future. No more Alpha children spawned from their blood, no more future leaders running their packs, and, if they merged, no Alpha child to rule what would become the largest pack in the US. He smirked cockily, realizing full well that he held sufficient power within his hands to fuck with the future of every single Wolven who had scorned him, and he reveled in it. Relished the fact that he was in control of their future and they didn't even realize it! His eyes flashed with glee, pleased enormously with the hypothetical outcome. Sure there were some pitfalls, but he'd deal with them as and when they came. It was wonderful to know that he held everything in the palm of his hand for once and he could and would crush it instantly, show no mercy to the bastards who had shown him no mercy, and he would enjoy every moment of it.

It all hinged on timing. If he took her now, then the packs wouldn't merge, his actions wouldn't influence the largest pack in the US. However, it would be easier to take her now, she wasn't on any of their pack lands and was, therefore, less protected. The effects of her abduction would be far-reaching either way, but he was a little unsure of when to do it. Allow the relationship to progress until the packs merged? Or take her now when it was easier? Tapping his fingers against his knee, he half-listened to their conversation and further planned out what his next course of action would be.

Either way, Kyle knew that in the long run they would find another Alpha to lead the packs or pack in the event of no heir, but he also knew how superstitious Wolven were. They liked a pack being led by one family, it made their pack look stronger to the outside world, made them more unified. They'd have to choose another Alpha out of sheer need, but no matter who it was, he wouldn't hold the same respect and wouldn't be looked upon as highly as a legitimate heir. Weaknesses would creep in and cracks would start to appear, mutiny was bound to happen, and the disunited and divided packs would unravel. Turning three strong packs into three severely weakened ones would please him greatly.

On impulse he determined to snatch her within the next few days. It would be nice to attack the future of the largest pack in America, but he decided not to be too greedy and to let providence favor him. Either way, messing with the future heir of three packs was bound to cause problems within the Wolven nation and he was damned pleased to be the instigator of that. They deserved to be knocked of their high horse, deserved to suffer for casting him and many others like him out because of their small-mindedness. It was ridiculous to despise humans, to only accept them if the Fates chose them as mates. What about the untold number of children that, like him, had been the result of a one night stand? What about their futures? Didn't they deserve to live a wholesome pack life? Did they have to live a life filled with fear, scared to breathe in case they shifted into some beast in front of someone? How many people out there thought they were animals because they'd been unfortunate enough to have a Wolven as a father?

An eye for an eye. Well, they'd cast him and who knew how many like him out without a thought to his or their future, so he'd take away their own future and with as little compassion as they had shown him and those like him. He'd revel in their packs' destruction, enjoy every single second of it. Was he evil? Maybe. But vengeance was sweet, and he and the countless others deserved to be avenged. He would see to it.

* * * *

"She's crying because of the baby, right?" Shane asked, obviously confused.

"Yes, dumb-fuck. That and she thought we'd left her, catch up!" Caden sneered and cocked a brow as Shane flipped him the bird.

"Shut up both of you! I swear you're like a bunch of fucking kids sometimes. She's crying because she feels insecure, the source of that insecurity is probably varied, but that's the main reason why she's upset. It's up to us to change that, do you want your mate feeling insecure?"

"No," both men said vehemently in unison.

"Good, I should think not," Dante lectured sternly. "She obviously doesn't understand how important mates are to Wolven. She probably doesn't even understand what a mate is. I think we need to explain it to her, and I think we need to spend time with her separately, one so that she doesn't think we're just here to fuck her and lose ourselves in her body, and two so that she can get to know us as individuals. There's always the danger that she could come to prefer one of us, but I doubt it. I think these last few days have bonded her to us intrinsically. I don't think spending a few days separately with her will undo any of that bonding.

"At seeing her distress at the thought of us leaving her, I think we can safely say that she doesn't want to be without us. No matter what she says now to the contrary. Be warned that she could lash out. She feels insecure, probably hurt and confused about what the fuck is going on here. Try to control your beast. Any perceived rejection can be dealt with at a later date or even forgotten, anything she says now that could possibly piss your beast off needs to be ignored. Just let it glance off you, okay? The last thing we need is for one of us to partially shift and to freak her the fuck out!"

"Yeah, you're right, Dante, but, the real question is, do you ever get sick of being a smug bastard?" Caden asked. Before he could answer, he posed another question, "So who gets to go with her first?"

"Well in my smugness, I think I should be the first. I'll be able to handle her emotions better than either of you would." As the other two glared at him, he joked, "Are you forgetting who my current Alpha female is?" Mentioning the woman who currently handled the women in Dante's pack lightened the atmosphere considerably. The Alpha female was an emotional and sometimes crazy bitch, but she was fucking strong and had yet to be beaten in any challenges the female Betas threw at her.

"Fuck," Shane muttered, "he's right, Caden. If he can handle that bitch then he can deal with Emma."

Caden laughed and concurred, "Yeah, I think you can handle Emma, Dante. If you can handle Lucia then you can certainly calm our mate. Fuck I bet you'll be glad to get Lucia off your hands!"

"Yes," Dante murmured sardonically, "I think it's best if you stay outside tonight. Either of you have a problem with that?"

"Fuck! Can't we stay inside?" Shane grumbled.

"You're getting soft, bro," Dante teased then said more seriously, "Shane, how do you think your wolf will react when he hears what's going on in the bedroom?"

Shane sighed, "He'll take control. But our wolves are just going to have to get used to sharing, Dante, I don't see why we can't continue to do that now!"

"Shane, for fuck's sake, I've already told you that Emma doesn't need to see us when we're shifted or even partially shifted. She's already seen us challenging each other, which is possibly the worst thing she could have seen. She doesn't need to be reminded of how quick we are to fight. Plus what we are undoubtedly still freaks her out. Do you want that? I personally don't. I want her to grow accustomed to us as humans, then wolves. Maybe she won't react with fear when she sees us as wolves next time that way. I don't want the wolves to be linked with aggression in her mind. If she shrinks back from that part of us, how do you think our beast is going to react? It's going to go ape-shit. Now . . . do you still think you should stay inside?"

Shane rolled his eyes and said, "Caden's right, you are a know-it-all bastard!"

Dante grinned and winked, then walked through the busted front door to find his mate, leaving the two men to entertain themselves for the night ahead.

"Why can't I stop crying?" Emma cried out into the empty room. She lay supine on the bed, eyes blurred and staring at the ceiling. Tired of the waterfall of tears falling from her eyes, she felt like screaming in frustration. Whatever the hell was wrong with her was driving her up the wall! She couldn't stand all these changes that were happening inside of her and could only assume that Caden, Dante, and Shane were the root cause of it. Bastards.

Although she'd been wrong, they hadn't been leaving her, the thought that they eventually would made her heart shudder in her chest. How could she deal with that kind of pain? Was it even worth it if she reacted to everything in this over-emotional way? She hated this, hated how she had been today. Ever since waking she felt as though she had over-reacted to everything. She was a scientist, had taught herself and had been educated to deal with things clinically and in a calm methodical manner. Everything that had happened today went completely against that. Did she really want this in her life?

Blowing out a sigh, she realized that the woman wanted them, the scientist didn't. The woman in her had started to love them and knew that they could become the focal point of her life. The scientist in her was shrewd enough to realize this as well and knew that the pheromone would no longer take center stage and that the men would become the very center of her being. With a strong urge to roll her eyes, Emma told herself that maybe she could have the best of both worlds. She would just have to deal with them a little more coolly, not allow them to control her or ride roughshod over her wishes. She had to make herself heard in this relationship, especially with the three of them. If she let them, they would easily take control of her life and she wouldn't, couldn't allow that. It would kill the strong independent person inside of her, and it went completely against the grain to allow her own character and personality to be overwhelmed by someone else. They were each so strong, she knew that it could happen easily if she herself didn't act accordingly and with equal fortitude. She knew that once she established herself in this relationship, it wouldn't be a problem, but these last few days, she'd allowed them to be in charge. She couldn't afford to let that happen anymore, so while a part of her enjoyed their domination, their complete mastery over her and her body, she couldn't allow it to happen each and every time she was with them. There had to be some give and take, otherwise she would lose herself in them and become a shadow of her former self.

It was bizarre, but she had never even contemplated the relationship splitting up so that she would be in what society considered a normal relationship. In her mind it was all three of them or nothing at all. She wasn't sure how she felt about that. Wasn't it a little weird to be so accepting of a ménage à quatre, for goodness sake? Was she weird to want to be a part of that kind of relationship? She didn't know. She just knew that even though it went against the scientist in hers wishes, the woman couldn't let any of them go. She'd be with them for as long as they wanted and would enjoy every moment of it, because today had taught her that she wasn't ready for them to leave her yet. That they would eventually go was a given. She knew it would happen, she just hoped it wasn't for a long while yet.

Focused as she was on herself, she was surprised that she heard the bedroom door open at all. She showed little reaction. Her eyes fluttered a little, but she didn't move, just continued to lay on the bed in wait for one of them to speak. Hearing a solitary pair of footsteps, her eyebrows shot up in surprise and her mouth turned into a little frown as she wondered what the hell they were up to.

"Do you understand what a mate is?" Dante asked calmly.

"I can imagine," she sighed wearily, turning on her side away from him.

"Emma," he said, giving an equally weary sigh.

She could hear the loaded tension in his voice.

"Please don't turn away from me . . . . I can't handle it very well."

Her eyebrows shot up once more in shock. She rolled over to face him and scowled, "What the hell do you mean by that? I can do whatever the hell I want, Dante!"

With a little grimace, he shrugged his shoulders then scratched his eyebrow with a tapered forefinger. Even annoyed at him, she couldn't help but recognize and appreciate his masculine beauty. She wanted to stare at him, take every little detail and absorb it into her memory. It still seemed so incredible to her that this man wanted her!

"It's a little difficult to explain."

She jumped a little at his words, as they jolted into the investigation her eyes were making of him. She smiled sheepishly at his questioning frown and sighed a little in relief as he continued.

"It feels like rejection."

"What?" she laughed mockingly. "Me turning on my side is rejecting you?"

"You're my mate," he answered simply. "You're turning away means you don't want to face me, that to me is rejection."

Coloring a little at his words, Emma mumbled, "I don't want to talk about being your mate."

Grasping her chin between his thumb and forefinger, he raised her head until her eyes looked into his. "You'll have to talk about it soon, Emma. We can't keep on ignoring this, especially after today, after your reaction to us going for a run."

He pointed it out a little cruelly, she thought, and blushed at his words.

He sighed and murmured, "We'll talk about this later, maybe tomorrow, but know that I wanted to deal with this now, okay?"

She nodded and whispered, "Thank you."

"You're welcome. What would you like to talk about instead?"

"Does it hurt when you turn into a wolf?" she asked, clutching at straws a little in her determination to change the subject.

He laughed and grinned, his sometimes somber face denying the charge as a boyish carefree grin lit his visage. "No, it's uncomfortable, but the most dominant emotion is one of freedom. I wish you could experience it for yourself, but you can't," he said, giving a sad smile.

She fidgeted a little. "Does it bother you that I can't?"

"No," he said softly. "I just wish you could know the freedom of it, that's all. I won't go too deep into it because you don't want me to, but you're my mate, Emma. It would take a lot more than that to bother me."

"I'm glad," she said with a smile. "When did you first change?"

"When I was twelve. That's pretty young to shift for the first time. Normally it's about fourteen for boys and about fifteen for girls. But Alphas shift earlier than their peers. It's the first sign of a child's future role in the pack. If you shift early, you know you'll be Alpha. Very rarely is more than one Alpha born in one generation, a handful of Betas sure, but the rest are just your everyday Wolven."

She snorted at that last part, but he just laughed.

"How did you come to know Shane and Caden?" Emma asked with interest.

"May I lie beside you?" he questioned politely.

"Sure," she shrugged, waiting for him to lay beside her, then, unable to help herself, she snuggled into his side. Hearing him sigh in pleasure, she hid a smile and took comfort in his presence and in his voice as he continued.

"Shane and Caden are the Alphas of two packs that border my own. My grandfather feuded with their grandfathers. It was a feud that spanned all three packs, then unexpectedly my father discovered he was mated to one of Caden's aunts. Shane's father was also mated to one of his aunts and to complicate and intertwine the packs even more, Caden's father was mated to one of my aunts," he laughed. "It nipped the feud in the butt instantly. The Fates work in mysterious ways, but, because we're all related, we've pretty much grown up together. They're more like brothers to me though than cousins or even friends. Seems like it's a good job seeing that we're sharing a mate," he joked, but on feeling her stiffen within his hold, he whispered, "Don't get all tense on me, Emma, just stating the truth." He pressed a kiss into her hair and tightened his arms about her.

Blowing out a breath, she whispered, "Know what frightens me?"

"What?" he murmured against her hair.

"I could lose myself in you, all of you," she answered honestly.

"Emma, the Fates wouldn't have chosen you unless you could handle us. So don't fear that. Look at how they worked their miracle upon our packs. At one point, in less-modern times, if someone from my pack had come across someone from Caden's pack, they would have tried to kill each other. Now harmony reigns among us because we're all linked by family. Why shouldn't this be the reason behind that? The Fates have determined that we three should share you, that our packs should be merged by the three Alphas sharing a mate. Who would have thought it, huh? In itself, that's shocking, but imagine how shocking it

would have been if we'd have all hated each other!
The world works in mysterious ways, Emma. Never
fear you'll get lost in us. You think we want that? Of
course, we don't! We want you, the *real* you!"
Spinning her more fully into his arms, he raised her so
that their heads were level and said forcefully, "I *want*
you!"

She saw the truth in his eyes and realized that he did
want her for her. For the most part she felt a little
relieved, but she knew that they wouldn't overpower
her purposely. They were Alphas, used to leading and
being charge, they wouldn't be able to help it. With a
sigh, she impulsively leaned down and pressed a kiss
against his lips. She felt him smile and felt the
vibrations as he whispered, "Don't think you can
distract me with sex, Emma."

She laughed and whispered back, "I'm not!" But
slipped her tongue out and along his bottom lip, sliding
it over the fleshy morsel and up to lick the upper one
as well as his came out to catch her own, she closed
her eyes on a sigh of pleasure as he dragged his tongue
down over her nerve-packed muscle. A slight shudder
worked its way through her when his hands came up to
rest upon her upper and lower back, pressing her down
against his firm hard flesh, nudging her belly with his
hardness. With a primitive and emotional moan, she
separated their mouths and their bodies to sit up,
quickly stripping her body of the shirt she'd dragged on
earlier and shrugging out of the trousers that adorned
her legs, she returned to his arms partially nude.

Both of them moaned as their flesh touched for the
first time. Emma spread her legs and cupped his
thighs with them, inadvertently bringing her pussy up
to nudge his cock. A shiver quaked over her at that
first touch. She rocked her ups. The friction drove her
slightly mad. She could feel him through her panties.
His hardness brushed all the right places, but it didn't
brush it enough, it was infinitely infuriating but at the
same time was all she needed. At this moment, it was

enough to touch him, to be touched by him, for their mouths to be their only connection. It was wonderful to kiss this man and know that he wanted her, that his cock was hard for her and even though it still astounded her, she no longer cared. She just wanted to revel in his touch, to revel in being so close to him.

His hands slid over her back, raising goose-bumps along the way and making her press herself even further into him. He groaned a little as she moved away from his mouth and kissed his jaw line, his chin, licked his earlobe, and suckled it into her mouth. When he reciprocated, they both laughed easily as they nudged each other's noses and banged chins in their desire to touch one another.

It was a revelation to Emma, who'd never had a lot of experience with sex. It didn't matter that she'd been treated to one large master class by three of the most sexiest and lust-inspiring men on the planet, she was still a novice, and being one on one with Dante seemed to highlight that fact to her. The touches were more intimate, more personal, the attention focused solely on her, not on how they could all touch her, how they could all pleasure and be pleasured by her. She supposed what *pleased* her was that she herself could devote more time to Dante. Before, she'd been at the very center of the three men, she received all the attention ,and, although she was a little unused to it, she had to admit that she enjoyed it. That she was coming to expect it, and, although it shocked her a little at how easily she'd capitulated to this alternative and unusual lifestyle and sexual relationship, she'd grown past caring. In reality, she had never lived an exactly normal life. Why should things change now.

No, what she was enjoying about this was touching him and only him, for Dante to be the center of attention, for her lavish him with her caresses. That was probably why she was a little nervous, having to caress him brought up an interesting dilemma for her. Once more her inexperience seemed way ahead of her desire. She wanted so much for him to *feel* wonderful, but she wasn't sure of how to do it. But being able to kiss him just for the sake of kissing him, just as a demonstration of her joy in being with him and his with her, was truly wonderful and a whole new aspect to love-making. It cheered her up some, took her focus from her nerves and back to just enjoying being with him.

Sighing against his jaw, her nose pressed into his skin, she whispered, "Why do you smell so damned good?"

He laughed but replied, "Why do you?" Rubbing his nose against her own jaw, they both sighed in mutual pleasure at the other's scent.

Pointing her tongue, she dragged it along the cords of his neck and back up again, enjoying not only his smell but his taste as well. Biting him slightly, she felt him shudder under her, and, unable to help herself, her hands spread out wide, tips pointed down so her nails dragged against his hard flesh. Pushing down hard, she watched as rivulets of red skin raised under her touch, saw the desire flaring in his eyes, and felt his cock quiver against her. A feeling of power overcame her, and it was in such a complete contrast to how she'd been feeling a little earlier, she became a little punch drunk. Leaning down to bite around his nipple, satisfied she'd left a mark when she studied the area more deeply. Tilting her head, she looked at him, and, even though she didn't want to say it, even though only thirty minutes earlier she hadn't wanted to talk about their relationship, unable to help herself, she whispered fiercely, her eyes flashing, "Mine!"

His eyes flashed back at hers, and somehow she recognized that her fierceness turned him on, that her possessiveness pleased him immensely. Climbing off him to stand beside the bed, she removed her bra and panties and climbed astride him once more, ensuring her pussy was positioned directly above his cock. With a buzz of power rushing through her system, she grabbed his hand and placed it in between her legs, using his fingers, directing them with her own, she touched herself, rubbed her clit with his callused fingertips, penetrated herself with his blunt and thick digits. Working herself into a frenzy under their dual touch, she groaned a little then moved his fingers away and, eyes staring into his, brought his drenched fingers to his mouth to sup at her juices, watching as he licked and sucked his fingers clean. She delighted in the burning look in his gaze, felt almost seared by it, and her body rejoiced at this display of his pleasure. It felt almost primal, as though she were claiming him and he, her.

Flinging herself beside him on the bed, she reached for him and when he was positioned between her spread legs, she gave a sigh of wonder, feeling his weight pressing her down into the mattress, feeling so encompassed in him, so surrounded by him, was just beautiful. Spreading her legs a little wider so that she could place her feet flat on the bed, she used the position to tilt her hips and as his mouth worked against her own, she teased them both with these little inconsequential and basically need-inspiring movements. She whimpered as he flung himself away from her. Kneeling now in between her thighs, she wondered what he was doing but then realized the way her body lay on the bed was perfect for what he was obviously intending to do next.

Holding his cock in one hand, he thrust the head inside her channel, just a little bit. Enough to drive her cunt mad, enough to not satisfy her at all. Despite herself, her internal muscles fluttered and clutched at him, and she groaned when he pushed all the way in and slowly but determinedly all the way out. Giving another whimper of need this time, her empty pussy hungry for him, she clenched her eyes as she watched him go through the motions again, his eyes focused on her cunt as it swallowed him deep. This time he just rested the head inside her and his eyes flickered up to her breasts, which wobbled under the intensity of her chest's movements, her breathing hurried and rapid as darts of pleasure and a need to be satisfied overtook her system.

"Pinch your nipples," he growled, his eyes flashing in warning as she was slow to obey, then smiling in pleasure as he watched her fondle the little nubs. "Do you want my cock, my mate?"

His voice was like gravel, it scratched her flesh, leaving her feeling red raw, and, God help her, ready!

"Yes," she moaned as her head tilted back helplessly.

"Say the words!" he demanded.

"I want your cock," she whispered hungrily.

"Repeat my words, Emma!" he ordered.

Wide open eyes looked at him in confusion, then clenching them shut, she realized what he wanted her to say, frowning a little, she said in a small voice, "I want your cock, *mate.*"

He teased her a little more, pulling out before pressing himself inside her, but when she whimpered as he made to pull out again, he shocked her by thrusting in deep, pressing their groins close together, as close as they could possibly go. Gasping at the suddenness of his penetration, she groaned as she felt his hard cock nudge all the little nerve-endings that loved to be touched, that worked her up and up until she would eventually climaxed.

Grabbing her hips to keep them high above the bed and continuing to kneel, he worked his cock inside her, thrusting by pushing her hips away and closer to him. It was a sensational feeling, one that made her focus almost entirely upon where they joined and one that pressed him even deeper.

Allowing him control, having relinquished it when she'd climbed off of him, she flung herself into abandon, her body focused inwards, feeling the rasp of hardness against her softest part, feeling the bluntness knock warm giving flesh sky-rocketed her need until she was whimpering continuously. Her eyes were blind as he plunged in and out of her pussy and drove himself into a frenzy simultaneously. She groaned as his hips worked harder, faster, and, with a silent scream, an orgasm rushed through her veins, so pleasurable it was painful. She closed her eyes against it, scrunched her face as though she were indeed in pain. Finally a hoarse cry escaped her mouth as the pleasure dragged on and on, lighting up darkened places in her soul it was so intense. Feeling the splash of his cum hit the walls of her pussy, his weight pressing her down into the bed as he collapsed upon her, these were the final sensations that bombarded her as her subconscious protected itself by fading her into sleep.

Chapter Six

With a groan of pleasure, Emma stretched against the rumpled sheets like a contented cat. The thought made her smile a little, because God, did she feel contented. She imagined that any cat that felt so damned good had to be basking in the sunshine on a warm summer's day and had just consumed gallons and gallons of cream and pounds of fresh tuna! Smirking, she scrubbed her face lazily with the back of her hand, murmuring a little dazedly as she recalled the intense dream she'd been having. Unable to help herself, a naughty grin graced her mouth as she remembered the very detailed and explicit story that had taken over her subconscious during the night. It was crazy, but she felt as though she'd lived it, had lived every second of that dream, experienced every moment; could, in fact, even feel the little twinges and the small unused aching muscles caused by a hot night of passion. Smiling a little at the thought, because she hadn't a clue of how a night of passion actually felt; she remembered on a sigh the feel of her dream guy's cock as it slid deep, thrusting its way past clinging rings of muscle into her ready pussy. The very intensity of that sensation made a bloom of a blush turn her flesh a rosy tinge of pink.

God, it had felt wonderful, so damn wonderful to be touched like that. So incredible that it seemed heavenly, not for ordinary mortals. For her body had felt as though it were being worshiped, her skin, its taste, its texture, everything about it had been savored, like a rare wine to be supped at and studied rather than gulped down like cheap cider. Never had she felt anything more luxurious, more wondrous.

With a sad smile that made her feel pathetic, she realized that it hadn't actually happened, she'd never actually been worshiped or savored like a rare vintage.

It had been a dream, nothing more, nothing less. The thought made her eyes pop open, and, squinting into the bright room, she scowled at the unfairness of life, to experience and remember all that in a dream was unjust. She knew that she would never be able to forget it, that it would forever be in her memory, and that was just cruel! To experience something so wonderful in a dream surely meant that it would never happen in real life. It would forever be a fantasy, nothing more, nothing less.

Stretching her back once more, Emma sighed and thought about how intense her work schedule had been, the dream must have been a sign that she'd been working too hard. Never had she experienced such an intense dream, and for this one to overcome her during the night, out of the blue and at a stressful time when all her experiments were finally coming together, merely meant that she needed to sleep more, needed to relax and stop working so hard. Hell, werewolves and long nights of passion and not just one hunky man drooling over her but a trio of them! She blew out a breath and realized that maybe it was time she had a break and rested before continuing with her work. To dream so deeply surely proved that she was nearing overload and that was the last thing she wanted, especially when she was so damned close to having the perfect pheromone!

Blowing out a breath, she made to sit up when a hand slipped over the skin of her belly and pressed her gently back into the sheets. Somehow managing to withhold a squeak of alarm, she spun her head around to face the hand's owner and nearly died of fright as she realized that this man was one of the main stars in her wet dream. Which meant that it hadn't been a dream. It had all been real. And werewolves did exist, and they did hanker after her body, and they did think that she was their mate!

Gulping, she watched as the man's eyes blearily opened, squinting against the sunshine, he smiled openly at her, which for some reason made the tension seep easily from her body, and when he pressed against her side, she easily rolled close to him, resting herself against him on a sigh of remembrance. It seemed so crazy to go from thinking he was a dream to actually waking up next to him, but the contrast was so wonderful she couldn't help but be relieved. To wake up thinking that the last few days had all been unreal had been awful! To never have truly experienced what she had was more of a nightmare than anything pleasurable. As he pressed a kiss to the top of her head, she snuggled deeper into his side and breathed a sigh of relief. "Dante . . . ." She was thankful that he was here, beside her in bed, and not just a figment of a horny, exhausted, stressed woman's subconscious.

She heard the smile in his voice as he replied on a yawn, "Yes, mate?"

"You're not a dream, are you?"

He laughed, not unkindly, but in a burst of surprise and confusion, "No, I don't think I am." His hand slid over her stomach. "You don't feel much like a dream either, thank the Gods!"

His callused palm brushed teasingly against her soft skin, making her tremble, and as he reached up to cup a breast, a slight shudder racked her frame. It was so wonderful to be touched by this man that she just lay there, allowing his warm hand to caress her and his other to chuck her under the chin until she tilted her head back in glad surrender, whimpering softly as he pressed a soft tender and loving kiss to her mouth.

Trailing his tongue along the line of her lips, he prodded the central rosebud of her mouth and grinned wolfishly as she allowed him entry, she felt the grin against her lower jaw and smiled back as their tongues slid alongside the other, raking goose flesh along her arms and upper chest. Her breath hitching in her throat, she arched her back helplessly and pressed the front of her body harder against his. Rubbing her nipples against his muscled flesh was an exquisite kind of pleasure that both teased and soothed the ache that had begun to overtake her body. Her feelings for him were as relentless as the sun beating down on the Earth, her body's responses perfectly natural in answer to his loving touch.

It was heavenly to caress him like this, to stroke and pet him, knowing that he was real, that he was hers. There was no urgency behind it, no dire need to make love. It was a simple thing, the need to touch to make sure this was all real had overtaken them both, and it was so indulgently satisfying that a sigh of wonder escaped her mouth.

Murmuring against her lips, he whispered in reflection of her earlier question, "You're not a dream, are you?"

Nuzzling her face against his, she whispered lovingly and on a huff of laughter, "No." Then, after pressing another soft kiss onto his mouth, she started to sit up, and, stretching once more, she realized something, and, God help her, the feelings from the day before were quick to rise to the surface. With a little alarm, she asked, "Where are Shane and Caden?" Feeling him tense, she had to stop herself from trembling and dropped herself down and rested upon her elbow. Looking at him with a frown, she breathed, "What's the matter?"

He smiled stiffly. "Nothing. I think they're outside."

A rush of relief that both relieved and annoyed her swept through her. They hadn't left her. Coolly, she tried to act as though nothing had happened, that those awful feelings from yesterday that she'd vowed to control hadn't nearly overwhelmed her. Raising a brow, she muttered, "Why on earth are they outside?"

"So we could spend some time together," he added a little sheepishly.

Frowning, she pulled away from him with a little nod, but was relieved at the simplicity of his answer. She knew he was telling the truth. And. to be honest, she had enjoyed being with him and just him. But not knowing where the other two were had frightened her more than she cared, and she realized that she had to stop it, had to control these feelings before they smothered her.   Heading towards the closet, she replied a little starkly, "I suppose that makes sense to you three.   Why do I always feel like I'm in the dark where you are concerned?"

"Maybe because you don't want to hear the truth," Dante answered honestly.

He was annoyed at her. It was evident in his tone.

"You can't deny that yesterday I told you that I wanted to let you in on everything.   I asked you to remember that I wanted to share everything with you and that it was your choice to procrastinate.   If you find yourself in the dark, then it's your fault, mate." On that last sentence, he rolled away from the bed and said quietly, "I'm going to find my cousins."

She tisked in the closet, finding it both amusing and a little tiring that he was peeved at her when he and his cousins had turned her whole damned life upside down. *He* had the audacity to be annoyed. She shook her head impatiently before grabbing a fresh pair of pants and a clean shirt. As he'd kissed and caressed her, she had felt the usual daze of pleasure engulf her, but the memories of the day before and her reaction to realizing Caden and Shane weren't with her had taken all pleasure from her system.

She didn't like how dependent on them she'd become, didn't like her reaction to their leaving. It shocked and appalled her that she could have reacted so extremely to something as simple as their going for a run. Whether they were telling the truth or not didn't matter. Just watching them run from her had felt as though a knife was being stabbed in her heart. That dependency scared her.   She didn't believe that she would be able to separate herself from them out of choice, even in self-defense, but she knew that she could use work as a focus to keep her brain functioning normally, for a little while at least! It had always worked in the past, and she didn't doubt that it would work now. Whether they were staying for the next week or the next few years, she had to grow some balls and become more independent. She was used to her own company, didn't relish the fact that that had changed within the space of three days! When they walked away from her, which she didn't doubt they would, she would have to be able to cope with their going. She couldn't just crumble into dust and wait for death!

No, she determined with a huff, she was going to start on her work again, restart her old life, and, with a start of guilt, she realized that she'd left the she-wolf caged in the woods for the last three days! Hurriedly grabbing her clothes, she raced to the shower to quickly freshen up.

* * * *

"Did you manage to tell her what she is to us?" Caden asked, his mood sour from an uncomfortable night spent roaming about. First he'd stayed close to the house, then he'd heard Dante and Emma together. The man in him had refused to join in, had respected what Dante was doing and because of that, his wolf had made sure he'd had a hell of a night.

"No, she didn't want to know. I think she's pissed off about something, not sure what though. Who knows with women?" Dante shrugged his shoulders, trying for nonchalance.

But both Caden and Shane could see he was tense.

"What's the matter?" Shane asked with a frown.

"I don't know," Dante said, sighing heavily. "Her mood just switched, like that," he said, clicking his forefinger and thumb together. "It was strange. She was happy and then, out of nowhere, she was really *un*happy!"

"Who's spending tonight with her? We'll either have to tell her today or the person who's with her tonight will have to do it," Shane said easily.

"I doubt she'll be any more open to either one of you discussing it with her. It was like talking to a brick wall," Dante protested.

Caden rolled his eyes. "It's not about ego, Dante. Yesterday she was probably just overcome with all the emotions hitting her. You didn't see her in the car. "

He huffed a sour laugh. "It's easy to understand if she's set up defenses. She's probably feeling very insecure."

"Yeah, I suppose, but still, I told her last night that I would answer any and every question she had, so what does she do? She blanks it so I tell her not to forget that I was willing to tell her. Then this morning, she throws it in my face that we keep her in the dark! Can you believe that?"

Each man sat squatting on the floor, butts perched on their heels, and Shane propped a hand in front of him as he blew out a breath. "Well, it can't be good for her, all those emotions rolling around her system. Not only is she pregnant, but she's pregnant to Wolven and newly-mated. It's no wonder she's up and down like a roller coaster. We need to take all that into consideration when we're dealing with her. I get why you're annoyed, but if her emotions and hormones are fucking with her, then we'll just have to get used to it."

"I think it best then if Caden stayed with her tonight, Shane. If sensitivity is what she needs, then he's usually pretty gentle and open."

"Fuck off, Dante, I can be sensitive too! Especially where my mate is concerned!" Shane growled, his mood souring in an instant.

"Look, don't start. It was merely a suggestion!" Dante sighed tiredly. "And the truth!"

Shane jumped up easily on to his feet. "Dante, it's all very well for you to sit here and preach after spending the night with our mate when Caden and I have been out here in the fucking forest, so just back the fuck off," he finished on a warning.

Dante laughed nastily. "Maybe you should take your aggression out on Caden, determine who's to spend the night with Emma by another challenge! Seeing as I can't even suggest something simple without you breathing down my fucking neck! It's the god damned truth and you know it, so stop being such a fucking prick!"

"If I was going to start on anyone, it would be you!"

Caden jumped up from his heels and on to his feet then pressed a hand to Shane's chest. "Calm down, Shane, this won't do any of us any good. Bear in mind that it's Emma that is important here, no one else."

"I know, but as usual he's being a complete jerk-off!" Narrowing his eyes at Dante, he sneered, "It's a role you take up often, cousin! Too often!"

Dante sighed and rolled to his feet. "Emma's coming."

"What?" Caden and Shane asked in unison, their heads spinning around to face the cabin as they sprung apart, watching a little guiltily as their mate quickly stomped over towards them.

"What the hell are you arguing about now?" she asked, annoyance evident in her tone and stance as she stood with her hands on hips.

"Why is everyone so aggressive today?" Caden asked smoothly.

"I'm not being aggressive! I just want to know what the hell is going on! First you're not there when I wake up, then you're arguing! All I ever seem to do is watch you all fight!"

"Well, that certainly makes a change from yesterday. I tried to tell you everything, but would you listen? No!" Dante replied angrily.

Huffing out a breath, she ignored Dante's comments then turned to face Caden and Shane respectively. "I gather if he wanted to spend time with me yesterday, it's one of you two's turn tonight! Well if that's what you're arguing about and are about to turn into dogs to determine who gets a piece of ass tonight, you can just stop it right now! I don't want either of you coming to my bedroom! I've got work to do, and it will take up a lot of my day *and* night. I won't have time for either of you!" Lifting her satchel up and pressing it against her chest like a shield, she walked away from the cluster of men with her nose held high in the air.

"Told you she was moody," Dante replied dourly.

"And I told you it's perfectly understandable why she is!" Caden answered him.

"Yeah, I suppose, at least we know why she was pissed now. She was scared when you weren't there. Suppose that makes sense after yesterday," Dante answered.

"Look, Shane," Caden said soothingly, "Obviously you're as temperamental as Emma. I'd normally suggest that two temperamental people don't mix! But in this case, your beast will take over, so you spend tonight with her and today we'll try to ease her mood, maybe even help her with her work," he finished easily. "Are we all agreed to make this day as easy as possible for her? If she'll let us, that is," he amended.

"Yeah," the other two replied in unison.

"That means no thinking with your cocks, either of you," Caden warned and grinned as they glowered at him before they all set off to find their pissed-off mate.

* * * *

Stomping through the woods she'd taken such pleasure in days earlier, Emma looked for the landmarks she needed to follow to return to the caged she-wolf. The difference in her mood was incredible. At this moment in time she couldn't imagine anything would make her feel better. She knew with a certainty that inhaling the scent of the woods deeply into her lungs wouldn't help at all!

She had no real idea why she was in such a bad mood. Dante had been perfectly correct when he'd told her that he'd been willing to tell her everything the night before, that it was she who had stopped him. She hadn't awoken in the best way, believing everything that had happened over the last few days had been naught but a dream. But he'd sweetened her mood, but soon after that, annoyance had burst through her veins like a storm cloud spraying raindrops on her head. She literally seethed with emotion now, the momentum of annoyance at its peak.

Emma entered the clearing without even realizing it, stopping only when she saw the wolves congregating about the cage. Snarling and hissing at each other, the males were fighting for dominance, fighting to impress the female. It was obvious that the female, however, was both oblivious to the men and that she was getting rather annoyed at the situation, the she-wolf was pacing about the cage restlessly, transmitting her unhappiness easily to Emma. Feeling inordinately guilty, Emma pressed the button that would release her into the woods and watched on a sigh as immediately the she-wolf ran from the cage as though, Emma thought with a snort, the hounds of hell were after her. The fighting males stopped their brawling and paused in shock before running after the she-wolf in haste. Snarling at each other as one ran ahead, they pounced and attacked as they ran for the she-wolf, their frustration obviously at fever pitch. They were stronger and faster than the she-wolf, but their constant fighting slowed them down and allowed the female wolf to get ahead.

Grimacing as she watched the large numbers of wolves chasing after the she-wolf, Emma hoped that they wouldn't hurt her. Then on a sigh, Emma realized that she was probably used to it. Males of the animal kingdom weren't usually kind lovers. It went against their nature. Unable to help herself, she realized that that obviously didn't go for all animals. The mythological kind were caring lovers, and she had three of them! The mind boggled.

Tensing as she felt one of *her* men walk behind her, she sighed as he rubbed her shoulder, "Emma, darling, it's still not safe to be around these wolves. They need to rut. They're dangerous. It would be safer for you back at the cabin."

Despite her annoyance at him and the other two, she couldn't help but smile at his tone. Dante was so obviously trying to be courteous and not order her about. "Alright," she conceded. She wasn't stupid. The male wolves were obviously volatile, the weaker ones who hadn't managed to beat the dominant wolves were still roaming the clearing, their anger showing in their tensed bodies and clenched muscles. She knew that if there was a faint trace of the pheromone on her skin, she doubted it but it was possible, then they could come running after her, confusing her for the she-wolf. It was a scary thought, and immediately she spun around, saw the other two men, and together they returned hurriedly to her cabin.

Little was said on the walk home. They surrounded her, and, although her annoyance had settled somewhat, eased by their protective stances, she had notes to write up and didn't intend to spend the rest of her day pining over them or being mollycoddled by them. She fully intended to focus on her work and *nothing* else! Maybe proving to herself that she could just *be* without them would make her feel a lot better. Being so dependent really went against the grain.

Stepping up to the cabin door, she looked at the open and broken door with distaste and then spun around to glare at them in warning before walking into her home and towards her lab. She had no way of keeping them out, in truth had no real desire to keep them out. No, she wanted them inside her house but could only hope that they would leave her in peace. It was imperative that she focused on her work, focused on anything that wasn't them!

Sitting down with a huff on to her lab stool, she tried to settle down and write down her observations of the day's events. It had been interesting to see how the pheromone had still been working strong after three days and how the males had reacted to it. It obviously increased aggression, but then that could be because of the duration of time they had spent in close contact with the she-wolf. Rather like prick teasing for three whole long days! As she started to put pen to paper to note her observations, she heard a knock on her lab door and with a little more irritation than she felt yelled, "Go away!"

Tapping her foot in irritation and frustration at her situation, she waited for them to knock again. She knew instinctively that they would, and when they did, she jumped up and opened her door, trying not to hiss as she said, "Yes?"

All three of them stood there watching her. For some odd reason it made her inordinately angry, and she glared at them before Caden said smoothly, "We have to talk, Emma."

"I don't want to talk! I want to be left alone! In peace to get on with my work! I have to write this stuff down before I forget it."

Caden sighed. "Well unfortunately for you, that's never going to happen, mate. We can't take no for an answer and no way in hell are we going to leave you alone!"

Grudgingly, she pushed past them, realizing that they wouldn't leave her alone until she listened to whatever they had to say to her. She walked into the living room, hands wrapped around her waist she stalked into the room and mumbled, "Let's get on with it then!"

"Sit down, darling," Shane whispered quietly. Walking over to her, he led her to the lone armchair. She allowed him to lead her and sat down with a little sigh. He perched on the edge of the chair and looked at her. "Emma, a few days ago you didn't believe us, thought we were mad when we came to you and told you that you were our mate. But it's too late now, you have to believe it because it's the truth. You are our mate and we are yours. You need to accept that, love. Please don't fight it," he finished gently.

Lowering her head, she stared at the hands she clasped at her knee, then mumbled, "It isn't that I don't believe you. I *believe* that you think I'm your mate. But I'm not, I-I, the wolves were crazy with lust for that she-wolf because of a pheromone I sprayed on her. It spilled on to me when I was dousing her in the scent. That's what attracted you to me. The pheromone. That's it. I'm not your mate." It was a relief to get that out in the open.

Dante gave a soft laugh. "Mate, don't you think we know this already? Of course we smelled the scent, but underneath was your own, the beautiful pure scent of our mate. Believe that because it's the truth. We won't lie, the pheromone attracted us to the scene.

Hell, it was impossible not to smell it on the she-wolf. It was damned strong, hellishly potent, but as we came closer, you were there and your scent overtook everything else. So you can stop thinking that what we feel for you is nothing but a chemical attraction. You're our other half, Emma. You must know this and realize what you are-our mate! Don't deny it, because denying it will only cause yourself and us heartbreak."

Closing her eyes against the need to believe, she whispered, "How can I believe this? It has to be the pheromone! Look at you three, look at me! How can you believe that I'm a match for one of you, never mind all three of you! It's impossible. Surely the Fates would never be so silly as to match us! It's implausible! You should be matched with someone more suitable. Instead you're supposedly mated to a mad scientist!" She shook her head wildly.

"It isn't, Emma," Caden told her quietly. "It's unusual, but it isn't implausible. You suit us. Maybe you can't understand how, but you do."

"Look, I'm not used to this! I'm a loner, for goodness sake! I live alone. I've done for years. I work all day, study the results of my work at night. I've dedicated my life to this pheromone. I have to keep on working on it. It's imperative. I just don't have time to have three mates!" she said, a little flustered.

"Don't you think we know that, Emma? For God's sake, we're Alphas, leaders of three of the largest packs in this country, and we're not saying that to impress you. It's the truth. Our packs are the most densely and heavily populated in America. Don't you think we lead busy lives as well! But when you meet your other half, exceptions have to be made! Surely you see that?" Dante asked testily, his earlier vow to be calm and supportive around her overly-emotional self blown out of the window!

"It just doesn't make any sense," she said, shaking her head in disbelief.

"Emma, it doesn't have to make sense. Last week, did you believe in werewolves? No," he answered for her. "You didn't, of course you didn't. Why should you? You were told they don't exist. Yet, here we are. It makes no sense, but we're still standing here! Soul mates don't exist, but here you are, standing in front of me, and you're my soul mate." Caden flung his hands out as if to say, Ta Da.

Rubbing a hand to her forehead, she muttered, "Alright, maybe I have to believe this. But I don't have to like it. You saw me yesterday, Caden! You saw how I reacted! I'm an independent woman, for God's sake! I've lived alone for all of my adult years, never relied on anyone, and yet, I was inconsolable over you going for a jog! I felt like I was dying because you were leaving me. That isn't normal. I don't want to live like that. I don't want to pine after three men!"

"Emma, it's the mate bond. If you tried to leave us, it would feel like dying to us, as well. Once mates meet, that's the way it is. We're soul mates. How do you think we're supposed to feel? Happy? Joyful at the prospect of our mate leaving us? Of course not. As strange as it seems, you acted rationally. We shouldn't have left you like that, not all of us at the same time. It was bound to shock you upon awakening. We just didn't realize you would wake up so soon."

"You can rationalize it all you want. It doesn't mean I have to like it," she burst out.

"No, it doesn't, but it does mean that you just have to get used to it! None of us have any choice in the matter and neither do you! We want you as our mate and hope you want us!"

She blew out a breath. "Okay, you're right, if you're stuck with me then I am with you! But just leave me alone to work, alright?" Climbing from the armchair, she didn't look back as she walked to the door. Pausing, she tapped her fingers against the wood and said a little uncomfortably, "Of course, I want you."

* * * *

Pouring a swirl of cream into the pasta dish she'd prepared, Emma divided the food out on to four plates and with a sigh of helpless frustration, recognized the emotion that was rushing through her. She couldn't ignore the pleasure she took in the thought of feeding and taking care of them, her mates. She wanted to roll her eyes in annoyance at herself, she'd told herself she was going to distance herself from them, but instead she gathered two of the plates into her hands and walked into the living room. All three men jumped to their feet as she entered the room and waited silently for her to speak as she passed one plate to Caden and then another to Dante. Returning to the kitchen, she grabbed the remaining plates and gave one to Shane, and, perching herself on to the edge of the armchair, she started to eat the meal she'd prepared.

Sighing heavily, she took a bite of the pasta and ate the meal quickly. It was nice, and she knew the men would enjoy it, but it could have been sawdust for all her palate enjoyed it. Saying nothing as the men conversed around her, she listened to what they were saying, concentrating more on that than on her food. They ignored her easily, Emma thought with a huff, as she heard them speak of what she supposed were pack politics. The names went over her head, but she could tell they were discussing something that was important, something about a rogue pack-whatever the hell that was!

As soon as she finished her food, she stood up and returned her dirty plate to the kitchen, leaving the men to talk and finish their food. Then she walked into her bedroom and easily started to strip off her clothes before getting into bed. Just looking outside her window told her it was late, that as per usual her work had dominated her mind. She couldn't help but be relieved. If they were her mates, if she had to feel so strongly for them, at least it wouldn't be to the detriment of her life's work. At least she wouldn't be thinking about them all day, every day. She had proven to herself that they wouldn't dominate her mind constantly, and she felt a lot happier and in a better mood because of it. Although she had said little over dinner, it wasn't because she was still annoyed at them, it was because the change of focus from work to food always knocked her a little loop. Her annoyance had simmered away over the day, boiling away into nothing. It was good to realize that that negative emotion had dried up and gone away, at least for now. She could sleep easily now.

Snuggling into bed, she napped a little before awakening as she had in the morning, to a warm body heating her back and hands sliding over her front, cupping her breasts and cupping her lower down. Squirming in his hold, she breathed deep on a particularly wonderful caress and realized that it was Shane behind her. "Shane, do something for me?" It was wonderful to awake to their touch. They always managed to sweep her mind clear of anything else. She didn't have to like it, but God help her, she loved them.

"Of course, Emma, what is it?" he whispered into her hair.

Hesitantly, she replied in hushed tones, embarrassed to ask but intrigued by the prospect of her thoughts, "Would you let me . . . ."

"Go on," he asked, curious as to her request.

"Can I watch you . . . touch yourself?"

Managing to withhold a chuckle of surprise, he nodded against her hair and said, "Turn the light on then."

She leaned over the side of the bed, twisted the dimmer switch so that a faint sheen of light shrouded the room. She moved back on to the bed and crawled closer to him. He was sprawled on the bed, an arm behind his head, legs lightly spread. She climbed over his legs and kept her eyes pinned to the hand that was resting on his right thigh. Sitting astride him, she leaned down and couldn't resist pressing a kiss to the head of his cock.

Teasingly, he asked, "You're sure you just want to watch?"

She smiled up at him. "I'm sure, can I help it if I

want to get involved every now and then?" Smoothing her hands along his hairy thighs, her eyes widened as she focused on him, giving him her whole attention. This little fantasy had been playing through her mind ever since the second day of having met them. She didn't know why, but she'd been longing to watch one of them, hell all of them, touch themselves. She could think of nothing more sexy than watching them jack off for her pleasure.

Licking her lips, her eyes focused on the hand that had edged closer to his cock, she watched with dazed eyes as Shane gripped himself tightly within his right fist. As it slowly moved up and down, she felt her breath hitch in her throat. Leaning forward she couldn't help but watch as his hand began to move faster and faster, dragging his foreskin over the length of his dick, rubbing and touching every single inch of skin as his fingers tightened at the base then swept over the now weeping glans. She sat astride his legs and spreading her own, she rode his left leg and moaned a little as her pussy brushed against his thigh. Dropping down, she lathed her tongue over the tip, cleaning his juices from him, savoring his taste, relishing that his taste belonged to her now and only her. The thought made her whimper in pleasure, she began to rock her hips, her pace matching the one that Shane used as he fisted himself and jerked himself to orgasm.

In awe, she watched as his hand moved faster, his eyes flickering as they focused on her wondering gaze, face and jaw tense with arousal. When long streams of cum shot from his cock, she gave a low moan of pleasure. His hand moved more feverishly now, milking himself of every drop, she watched as little spatters of semen splashed his belly, chest, and hips.

With dazed eyes, she watched him squeeze himself tightly, in such a grip that she thought would cause him pain, but, intrigued, she watched as the last drop of seed escaped the small slit and, whimpering, she lowered herself to his cock's level, fluttering the tip of her tongue against that last drop of seed. He groaned, obviously still sensitive, but she moved away, quickly roaming over his body, licking and supping at his cum, the cum that belonged to her.

Feeling insanely primitive, she reached for his hand and placing it between her legs, she directed his fingers with her own and rode herself to a quick and pleasing orgasm, that left her feeling energized. Rather an unusual feeling after the last few days when she'd taken to passing out after cumming!

Sprawling over his torso, she lay upon him in comfort, reveling in being touched by this man and knowing his most intimate secrets.

* * * *

The lapping of a tongue against her clit was her first wake-up call, feeling the flexible muscle actually curl around it made her skin quiver and her limbs tremble. Then pressing down, Shane licked it roughly, bringing her a little more to life and out of the world of sleep.

When he wrought a moan from her sleepy mouth, he crawled up her body and settled himself between her thighs, his cock brushing the tender flesh of her cunt. Resting it there between her pussy lips, he waited for her to become a little more alert. He smiled as she reacted to the heavy press of his dick against softly swollen tissues. Leaning down, he grabbed his cock in his fist and pressed the head into her. Lodging it in, he allowed her to accustom herself to his dick. Groaning a little as her muscles fluttered and played around him. Thrusting deeper, he pushed through the ring of muscle that tried to stop him and sighed wondrously as he hit home, hips flush to her pelvic bone, his cock as deep as physically possible.

Her eyelids fluttered in surprise at the feeling of fullness. She groaned as he moved, not in a thrust, but just in a movement to make himself more comfortable in the position he was in. The little jerk just added to that sensation of being absolutely filled, and, not knowing why, small teardrops clustered in her eyes and began to fall over her cheeks. When he leaned down to kiss them away, she grunted as this action caused a similar feeling to invade her. She felt consumed by him, and she both loved it and loathed it. It was a rather suffocating feeling yet at the same time liberating. Never had such contrasting emotions overtaken her!

Unsettling her from the spot she lay in, he pushed his arms underneath her torso and with brute strength, lifted her upwards and into his torso. Ignoring her whimper of alarm, he settled himself on his heels, then slowly on to his butt and smiled as the position brought her breasts into his line of sight.

"What did you do that for?" she moaned huskily, the feeling of impalement was complete, not an inch was spared, she was sure of it! Every nerve, every inch of tissue, everything was touched by his invading ruthless cock. Nothing was saved from its brand, and, God help her, she loved it. Ignoring her discomfort, she sat up and closed her eyes at the movement then, breathing in deep, she settled into the cradle of his legs, his thighs supported her back all the while.

"Why do you think?" he teased, then sat up a little to press small kisses to the crests of her breasts. Licking the nubs, he flickered his tongue along the dimpled skin, raising them to prominence. "You have beautiful breasts, mate." he growled primitively.

"Thank you," she whispered huskily.

"You accept it then," he asked roughly.

She didn't pretend to misunderstand, instead looked into his eyes and whispered, "Yes," looking down at his chest, she leaned forward to distract him, and it worked. His hands immediately came up to cup her breasts, jiggling them within his massive hands, hands that had earlier pleasured her to an orgasm, hands that had milked his cock of every last milliliter of cum. The thought made her eyes flare and her hips began to rock, just picturing that scene in her mind, seeing the small spurt of his seed escape its prison made her moan. She had no idea why it turned her on so, but it did and as her hips quickened, she used the strength in her thighs to ride him, to lift herself away from his cock and to use the weight of her body against her. Dragging him to the edge of her cunt then forcing him back forcefully into her depths.

The pace was punishing, hard on her tired body and hard on her over-worked nerve-endings. She could feel the exact instant when her body began to climax, a rainbow of colors dazzled behind her eyes. They drenched her in a sated sensation, one that both tired and energized. Each thrust, each impalement flung her farther into that rainbow. The splash of his seed inside her womb merely brightened the whole scene. Pressing herself down harshly against his cock, she screamed as the move made her legs split a little wider open, which unbalanced her enough to fall heavily on to him. Surges of energy traveled along every nerve-endings, frazzling and burning her as they scorched their path along each inch of her body. With a tired moan, she collapsed against her mate's chest, secure in the fact that he would protect and care for her, happy to place herself within his guard.

Chapter Seven

Her nose pressed into Shane's side, Emma inhaled deeply and delighted in the sheer unique essence of his skin. If it were possible, she would have tried to diffuse his scent into her very being. Each man had a different aroma and every single one of them made her stomach start to churn with need and desire. It was something only they inspired in her and something only they could quench.

The pheromones their body exuded were perfectly attuned to her olfactory senses. Just being in their presence was enough to start the fires burning in her center and now, laying beside one of them, embers banked, she sighed both in pleasure and comfort. Perhaps just being touched by him was enough to relax her, but she knew that she had never felt such peace than during these last days with these three men. At the same time, however, she'd never felt so turbulent, so out-of-control. It was such a bizarre contrast that she shook her head a little in surprise. From one end of the spectrum to another, they roused emotions and feelings in her that were immensely complex.

Whether they were her mates or not, she'd grown to love them in the inordinately short space of time she had known them. Perhaps it could be said that it wasn't love, just lust. And having so little experience, how could she determine between the two? Not only that, but how could she love not just one, but *three* men? But somewhere deep inside herself, she knew that this was how love felt. It burned brightly in her heart, made her soul glow in repletion. What she felt for Caden, Dante, and Shane could in no way be classified as just lust. It was richer, deeper, and far more precious than that. Like a rare jewel, it glittered brightly within her being. She knew that it would last a lifetime. She just doubted whether their 'love' for her would endure.

No matter how much they tried to persuade her differently, a part of her couldn't really believe in mates. She had listened to them intently, watched their earnest faces as they explained how important she was to them. But how could an educated woman and a trained scientist actually believe in soul mates? She blew out a gentle breath that lightly dusted his skin, making a river of goose flesh ripple over his torso. Stiffening slightly, aware that she could have awoken him, she made herself relax against him, allowed her limbs to go lax and was rewarded by a deep sighing inhalation.

Returning to her slightly disconcerting thoughts, she once again asked herself how a professional scientist could even believe in the concept of mates. But then, werewolves didn't exist either! Rolling her eyes because their existence was definitely a fact, she realized that she would just have to learn to trust them and believe in them. It was difficult but a necessity. She just had to believe that there was no reason for them to lie to her and every reason for them to be telling the truth. The cynic in her fought the caring woman and she wasn't truly sure who won the battle.

Determined to once more ignore her thoughts, she fought another battle and lost as, unable to help herself, unable to disallow herself the pleasure of touching him, she trailed her hand along the muscled planes of his torso., her fingers scoping out and seeking his warm flesh, trickling over his hard eight-pack. Closing her eyes, she almost felt like wiggling in delight. How did she, a geek, get a man with an eight-pack? It defied all belief, how could it not?

"Hmm," his voice was husky from disuse. "Good morning, Emma." His hand came up to catch hers and slowly he trailed it further down his body and lower so that her hand was covered by his and together they cupped his cock. She squeezed him gently then and as he groaned, his hips shifted slightly, making Emma tighten her grip on him. She closed her eyes in sheer delight at his reaction to her touch. That this man desired her made her whole body quiver contentedly, and, in response, she quickly climbed astride his thighs.

Shane's hands came up to clasp her waist then smoothed upwards to touch her breasts and tweak at her nipples. Undulating her hips against his, her eyes sparkled as with her free hand she reached for one of his and brought it down to her cunt. Closing her eyes as his fingers seemed to directly target her clit, she ground herself against him and moaned deeply. A feeling of abandon seemed to permeate her entire body and she loved it. Not for the first time during these last days together, she felt free and she reveled in it. It was like a drug, but then being with them was addictive, so there was no reason why being touched sexually by them would be any different!

Bending down over him, she trailed her breasts along the smoothness of his chest and pressed a closed kiss to his mouth, licking his lips with her own then trickling the tip over his jaw, neck, and collarbone. Nipping at his pec, she felt her eyes flash triumphantly as she managed to mark him and saw the reflective desire and lust that that branding caused. Grinning at him, she lifted herself, knocked his hand away, and pressed herself down on to his hard long cock.

Her eyes fluttered as the thickness of his dick plunged inside her, tickling every inch of her pussy. She shuddered at the feeling of fullness. "Fuck," she moaned gutturally and rolled her hips to push him deeper. Her hands came up to his chest, and she used his torso as leverage. Flexing her hips, she started to ride him, her breath starting to hitch and her face crumbling as pleasure battered against her as she slowly worked him in and out of her tightness. Clutching him with her inner muscles intensified every feeling tenfold until it reached the point where it became difficult to ride him. To feel the drag of his cock against her swollen inner tissues was unbearably intense. She couldn't help but cry out and sighed in relief as he rolled them over so that she lay beneath him.

His hips alternated between pummeling into hers then sliding in and out of her slowly. During those teasing moments his mouth lowered down to hers, pressing gentle kisses to her parted, gasping mouth. It was strange to feel as though she was being cherished then fucked. It excited her impossibly. His cock began to piston into her, driving her upwards and upwards. Her fingers sloped downwards and in between their sweating bodies. Scissoring down between her drenched pussy lips, she began to play with her clit, pushing down on the small button, she gave a cry of pleasure. The feeling of both deep penetration and manual stimulation made her shudder, and, as his pace quickened, she felt herself begin to drown in a tide of desire.

Moaning, her breath hitching, Emma felt the climax overtake her. It seemed incredible how that intense lust could translate itself so purely into her very being. Her body burned, and, as he moved to reach his own pleasure, small fireworks set off behind her eyes, hurting them in their glare. She felt suffocated in the blanket of bliss, gasping breaths escaped her tightened throat, and her fingers fumbled in the mass of her juices. Screaming aloud as the tornado of pleasure caught her in its eye, she shuddered and felt her mind slip away.

She awoke a few minutes later, her body wrapped up in Shane's arms. She found herself clinging to him shamelessly, exulting in his touch and wanting to be engulfed by him. She allowed herself a few minutes in his arms before she disentangled herself. "I have to work, Shane," she mumbled as she crawled out of bed, her legs a little shaky as she stood on both feet. She longed to remain in bed with him, but something held her back, pushed her to work, and, as always, she trusted that inner voice that had always guided her. How could she not listen to it now?

That pervading weakness seemed to hamper her slightly, but was that any wonder, after what she'd just been doing! Feeling a blush touch her cheeks at the thought, she wondered for a moment when and if she would ever stop feeling these damned flushes. Wondered whether she would ever be able to walk around without her seemingly ever-present rosy red cheeks!

Walking into her closet without looking back at him, she chose a simple pair of denim cutoffs and a white singlet vest. The top was a very masculine A-shirt, but it fitted her like a glove . She knew that it would turn the three men on, simply because it cupped her breasts like a glove, and, if she didn't wear a bra, her nipples would show through. Grabbing a pair of panties, she headed out of the bedroom and into the bathroom. Noticing along the way that he'd already left the bed.

As she brushed her teeth, she stared at her naked body for a moment. It was good, she supposed critically, the shape was good but nothing extraordinary. She would never be super-skinny, but she had some good curves. Looking into her bathroom mirror raised a few questions though. When she looked at herself she saw average. Looking at them, she saw an Adonis. Why would three Adonises choose her? Or if they had no say in the matter as they all said, why would the Fates choose her for them?

Feeling a little gloomy, she washed her face then stepped into the shower to wash herself. That damned hypersensitivity hadn't disappeared yet, but over the last few days her mind had been elsewhere and so she hadn't noticed it as much. Frowning as she realized that her ignoring it had seemingly made it go away to some degree, she damned herself for thinking about it. She swore when, standing under the spray, the harsh water drops flying against her tender skin made her mind float away a tad. It was back, thinking about it had brought it back. Damn!

Grimacing as she sat down on the shower floor, she grabbed the bottle of soap and poured some of it into the palm of her hand. Cringing, she quickly washed her intimate parts then dragged a hand over the rest of her body. Allowing the water to trickle down the faucet, she cupped some in her hands and smoothed it over her limbs, washing the suds away.

Once clean, she stood up with a scowl as she realized that she would once more have to ignore the towel. Firmly she brushed a tensed hand downwards to skim the excess water away. As she started to dress, she couldn't help but notice that the A-shirt clung even more than usual, her nipples peaked from the air brushing them were entirely prominent within the confines of her tight vest. Walking out of the door, she almost bumped into Shane. Hands on hips she glared at him and asked, "Why can't I shower anymore?"

Frowning, he stood around her and walked into the bathroom, testing the water he sent her a questioning glance. "It's working now, baby."

Pursing her lips at him, she couldn't stop scowling at him. "The plumbing is perfectly fine, Shane! Why can't I stand underneath the spray without feeling like I'm going to pass out?!"

"Ah," he grimaced, "Well, that could be something to do with our DNAs mixing. As you grow accustomed to us, it will go away."

His very earnestness pissed her off even further. Shooting him a murderous glance, she stalked away to her lab. Slamming the door shut, she began to pace the small confines of her workspace and glared at everything and anything. Tapping her foot on the floor, she pondered what he'd said. Could that be it? That her hypersensitivity was linked to their being Wolven? As she thought about it, it made sense, and, unable to help herself, she sighed out in relief. She had been starting to think something was really wrong with her, but the clash of their foreign DNA with her own was bound to have caused some issues in her body.

Obviously, they weren't overly concerned, they knew what was happening to her, well apart from the empathy. She hadn't told any of them about that, because it wasn't exactly concrete, was it? She found herself unwilling to believe in it, so why should they? All she knew was that around these three men, bizarre things were happening to her, and, God help her, she loved it.

Grimacing at the thought, she looked around her lab and sighed as she realized that she was going to get no work done. Opening her door, she walked into the kitchen and headed for the fridge. As she passed through the rooms, she noticed that none of them were inside. She could only assume that they were congregated outside. Unlike two days ago, the thought didn't terrify her. She knew that they wouldn't exactly abandon her now. Just thinking that made her feel a little better about the whole situation. She was beginning to trust them, little by little.

Searching through her almost-empty refrigerator, she grabbed the last dozen eggs, some ham, an onion, and the last chunk of cheese. Smashing the eggs into a big dish, she whipped them with a fork then set about slicing the ham finely and dicing the onion. Although she understood why onions made her cry, the explanation didn't stop her from damning them! As tears poured down her cheeks, she added the onion and the ham to the beaten eggs. Searching for her largest pan, she set it in the stove on a medium heat and added a knob of butter. Lowering the heat a notch, she poured the raw omelet into the pan and nodded as it began to sizzle as it touched the butter.

Leaving it to cook, she grabbed the utensils she'd already used, dumped them in the sink, and began to wash them up. Upon finishing, she set out four plates on the work surface then reached for salt and pepper. Heading back to the stove, she turned the omelet over and smiled at the golden brown egg dish. It was firming up nicely and would be cooked soon. Standing over the hot pan, she flushed as she realized how much she enjoyed cooking for them. Knowing how much to cook was a little difficult, she'd broken the entire dozen of eggs into that omelet and could only hope that that would be enough for them. She herself would only have a small slice, but they were large men and would surely eat a lot. Not only that, they were Wolven, that meant they'd eat even more, didn't it?

Pulling a face at the pan, she lifted the omelet with her spatula and peeked underneath then sighed in satisfaction. Cooked to perfection. Taking the pan off the heat, she divided the omelet into four then placed the smallest slice on her own plate and the other three on the remaining dishes. After sprinkling salt and pepper on top, she walked over to the kitchen window, opened it, and yelled out, "Caden, Shane, Dante! Breakfast is ready!" It wasn't long before she felt the vibrations of their feet in the hallway, and, placing the plates on the small breakfast table, she grabbed knives and forks and lay them beside the dishes.

When they came in and sat down, little was said between the four of them. The men conversed mostly between themselves and left her to herself. Standing up to eat as she was, she could watch them. It was nice to see them enjoy their meal, even better to watch them interact with one another. Sighing a little, she said into the sudden silence, "I've been meaning to head into town for a few days, as I'm running out of supplies."

Dante nodded. "We'll handle it." His voice was gruff, with a meaning behind it that she didn't really understand. Frowning slightly, she finished the last bite of her omelet, noticed that they'd finished also, and walked over to collect their plates. She was handed them without mishap and returned to the sink to wash them up. Without turning back, she heard them step away from the table and walk back down the hall. She was a little surprised that they hadn't thanked her for breakfast. However, on turning around, she released a soft sigh as she spied three beautiful wildflowers laying on the breakfast table. Drying her soapy hands, she walked to the table and picked up the two she recognized, one very delicate and called a cream cup, beautifully simple with a central spot of yellow set against the creamy background of the petal. Six of these were set around the cluster of stamens at the very center.

The other flower was called, rather appropriately, Purple Lupine. A long flower, she looked at it and supposed that it was rather triangular in shape, starting wider at the bottom before tapering off at the top. Clusters of purple petals were dotted around the lavender-colored flower, and she smiled at the lovely vibrant color.

The third plant was shaped rather like a star, five petals, each separate and not touching, gathered around the central cluster of stamens. Surrounding these stamens however were tinier versions of the flower, it was inordinately pretty and golden yellow in color.

Smiling at their gift, she looked at them and realized that they had to have looked about for these three different flowers, because a cream cup would definitely not be growing near a purple lupine. She was touched at the effort they had gone to for her sake. It was a simple gift, but it truly warmed her heart. She was also relieved to realize that the thought of them going into the woods didn't frighten her as it had done the other day. She truly was growing to trust them, for better or worse.

Laughing at the meaning behind those words, she searched in a cupboard for a long glass. Usually she wasn't a flowery person and actually didn't own a vase. So filling the bottom of a water glass with a little tap water, she popped all three flowers into it and smiled with pleasure at them. Reaching for the glass, she walked with it to her lab and set it on one of the work surfaces. It was hard to concentrate on her work when all she wanted to do was think about the three of them. But sitting down, she nodded resolutely and began to study the read-out that she'd printed last night and had meant to look at earlier this morning.

* * * *

Quickly jumping to her feet, Emma walked to the door and opened it. To be honest, it was a relief to be distracted. She'd hardly got any work done and had sat there half the morning scratching her head at some strange anomalies her test results had thrown out at her.

It was hard to stop the sigh of delight at Caden's nude body, she managed barely and made herself pull a straight face. Could she help it that these three men made her vision fog? No, she couldn't, and if they didn't want to be stared at, then they shouldn't walk around bare-assed all the time. After all, it just invited a girl to look, didn't it? "Yes, Caden?" she asked, tilting her head to the side in a move that took his cock away from her line of sight.

"There's some rabbits in the kitchen, just thought I'd let you know."

Emma frowned, a little perplexed, what the hell did he mean there were rabbits in her kitchen. "Rabbits?"

"Yeah, they're fresh," he replied earnestly.

"You mean there are dead rabbits . . . in my kitchen?"

"You said you needed supplies!"

Eyes a little glassy, she gulped and told him, "Caden, I . . . thank you, but I've never cooked anything *that* fresh. Does it still have its fur on?" she asked, shuddering a little at the thought.

"Of course, darling," he smiled and leaned down to press a kiss to her waiting mouth.

Unable to repress the small sigh of contentment, she closed her eyes for a second and dove in deep to his caress, only leaping out when he murmured, "Don't worry about the rabbit, I'll deal with it." He left her with a wink, and tossed at her, "I'll shout for you when it's ready."

Staring a little blankly at him, she left her door open so that she would be able to hear his call and returned to her desk. Between him leaving her and calling her for lunch, she managed once more to complete hardly any work. Jumping up at his shout, she slowed her pace down, not wanting to look as though she had been waiting on his call. A girl had to look busy, didn't she? On entering the kitchen, she noticed that all three were there again, but this time a plate had been set for her at the breakfast table. She settled between Shane and Dante, who were already seated and watched as Caden finished pouring what looked like a stew on to their plates.

Walking forward with two dishes, he placed one in front of her and the other in front of Shane then returned for the other two and placed it on his setting and Dante's. "This," he announced proudly, "is Coniglio all'Onegliese."

Shane chuckled heartily. "Did Larsia teach you it?"

Caden responded with a glare, "And what if she did? Is it a crime to learn a recipe?"

"No," Shane said, shrugging before adding on an aside to Emma, "Larsia is . . . well used to be his Alpha female."

"Alpha female? Used to be?"

"She rules the women and, I say used to because the alpha feel now is you. You're the leader of all the women of our packs."

"Me?" Emma squeaked. "I've never led anyone!"

"Doesn't matter," Dante said, shrugging before repeating, "The Fates wouldn't have chosen you unless you were fit to be Alpha female."

"I'm getting pretty sick of you telling me that, Dante. I don't give a shit what the Fates say. I've never led anyone before. I've never been a team leader or held a managerial position. You say you have the largest packs in the US, how the hell am I supposed to lead the women in them?"

"Don't worry about it, darling," Caden said, laughing at her irritation, "you have no idea how imperious you can be. You'll be fine."

Her brow furrowed in irritation as she looked at him before muttering, "Is that supposed to be a compliment?"

"I don't think that's necessary. You know how we feel about you. Anyway, stop shit stirring, Shane. There was no need to bring up Larsia, just eat what I've cooked and shut up," Caden warned with a nasty glare.

"Oh, don't start arguing, you all drive me crazy!" She sighed before taking a bite of the dish and moaned in delight at the taste. "Oh, Caden, it's delicious." She hid a smile as he preened a little.

"I'm glad you like it, mate. You needn't worry about supper either."

"Oh?"

He nodded his head to the counter, atop it lay a surprisingly large array of different vegetables, all fresh, she knew because soil littered the work surface. On another, lay some more rabbit, still in their skins. "There's enough for tonight and probably lunch as well. It's Dante's turn to cook this time though."

Her eyebrows shot up in surprise, but on thinking about it, she supposed it was their way of showing her that they were the provider and she couldn't deny that they had indeed done that! "Where did you get all the vegetables from?"

"We live off the land, mate. We're not animals," Dante said rather pointedly.

"Did I say you were? No, I just wondered where you could get all that food from! Why are you being so touchy?"

"I'm not, I know you're *still* not overly convinced that we are your mates. I don't want you thinking that we're animals at the same time we're trying to convince you of your importance in our lives!"

She sighed but said nothing, just took another bite of her meal, which tasted earthy and clean, yet simply beautiful and all at the same time! Quickly she ate her lunch, managed to savor the flavors despite her hurry. Upon finishing the meal, she stood and kissed Caden on the cheek before thanking him and walking back to her lab.

Finally she understood what the hell had happened with her experiments. The wolf she'd tested had just finished the last stage of her estrous cycle. She'd still been partially in heat! Dammit, it pissed her off that she hadn't picked the best test subject. Anomalies were bound to have been thrown out during the course of the experiments. How could she have overlooked the wolf's hormonal cycles?

Looking at it objectively didn't help either. She'd used the best available to her and now had to deal with the consequences. It meant that she'd have to do the fucking thing again, which was both a waste of her time and resources, and she had little of either! Especially since Caden, Shane, and Dante had come into her life. Now she had even less.

Nearly snorting at the thought, she blanked them once more from her mind, not wanting to distract herself from her work. She had finally managed to bombard herself sufficiently with her test results and the complications that had arisen to the extent that she'd finally been able to focus on something other than them and she didn't want it to stop!

She managed a good two more hours before she conceded defeat with a stretch and left her lab. She poked her nose into the living room, saw that it was empty, and headed to the kitchen. It was rather comical how overnight they'd seemingly vouched to persuade her of her status in their life via her stomach. She couldn't help the soft smile that touched her lips as walking in she saw Dante covered in flour and arguing with Shane about something.

"Dinner's nearly ready," Caden informed her, looking up from some papers in his hand.

Smiling, she whispered, "I think Dante's managed to get more of the dinner on him than on the plates!"

"The bag exploded on him. He deserved it," Caden shrugged.

She frowned at his weird comment, but she laughed as Dante glared at him. Obviously, it was a joke between the three of them as Shane laughed heartily.

It was rather a relief for them to do the cooking. She had to admit she wasn't adverse to their talents. How could she be? It meant that she didn't have to do it! She understood that they had primary motives in cooking for her, but she thought that, to some degree, it was pleasure in feeding her. She had felt the same way when cooking for them. Either way, she appreciated their taking over the kitchen. Ordinarily she would make a roast one day a week, then have sandwiches until all the meat was gone. Or she'd make a huge vat of soup and freeze it. She cooked for expediency, had always considered it time taken away from her work and had spent as little time as possible in the kitchen.

When Shane placed cutlery in front of her, she smiled at him and took a sip of Caden's water, which lay near the elbow he'd planted on the table. Then, as Dante placed her meal in front of her, she surreptitiously patted him on the leg in thanks. Seeing him jerk in response, she realized that it was one of the first times she had ever touched him voluntarily and in a non-sexual fashion. Averting her eyes, she started to eat her meal, roasted rabbit encrusted in herbs and garlic potatoes. She sighed in delight at this, another damned gorgeous meal. "Where did you guys learn to cook? This is beautiful."

Dante laughed. "Where do you think? Our mothers."

Cheeks tinged with a blush, she mumbled, "I never thought about you having mothers."

"We're not monsters, Emma," Caden said, sighing wearily.

"What is it with you three today? God, I can't say anything without you thinking I'm being offensive. I *meant* that I can't imagine you being children or being parented. I didn't mean it nastily, just that you all seem so . . . male. It's hard to imagine you as little boys."

"Like Dante said earlier, during this crucial time of your accepting us, we don't want you to discredit us with untrue beliefs," Shane answered her somberly.

"I don't understand why you think that. I'm not an idiot, although my last comment may have told you otherwise. Fundamentally, I actually am a scientist. I've seen some stuff these past few days that may have set my world on its head, but that hasn't made me a bigot or unfair. I will only think you're a bunch of bastards if you behave like a bunch of bastards. Innocent until proven guilty, I think is a good way of putting it," she said.

Caden laughed. "You know how we feel about you, Emma. We know how hesitant you are towards us. Don't you think that gives us the right to be a little touchy? We want you, Emma. It's as simple as that."

"I know, I know. But don't bite my head off every time I make a comment, or I might just stop talking! What were you reading earlier, Caden?" She made an effort to stop feeling resentful and changed the subject to what she hoped would be less turbulent ground.

"We returned to our packs this afternoon. The Elders gave me some information about the latest goings-on."

"The elders?"

"We're the Alphas, our rule is indomitable, but the oldest members of our pack sort of watch over us, make sure we don't become bloodthirsty heathens," he teased.

"Your watchdogs, I suppose."

"Yeah. I've had some problems with my Betas for

the past few months, they're getting restless, and the Elders were just keeping me in the know."

"What kind of problems?"

He shrugged. "Nothing serious. It's a habitual problem, comes with the territory. They want to be Alpha and I don't want them to be."

She nodded a little wryly. "It's strange because I know a lot about wolves and their pack interaction, so I understand the basics, but it's so different from anything else I've ever learned. This whole thing is quite amusing really and couldn't happen to a more appropriate person-a wolf expert. Does this happen in your packs, Dante? Shane?"

Shane replied first. "Of course it does baby. Like Caden said, it comes with the territory. Caden's unlucky, his pack has a lot of Betas. It means he's almost always got some bastard challenging him."

"Yeah, it's Derrick this time."

Dante groaned. "I swear, that guy is a moron. How many times has he challenged you now?"

"I think this is the fifth time," Caden answered wryly, then said to Emma, "Challenges are part of pack life, it's a way of ensuring that the Alpha is strong enough to lead the pack. With in-house challenges, the Elders approve of them so one egotistical prick can keep on challenging me because it stops me from growing stale."

She could tell this was a direct quote from one of the Elders and frowned. "Do you get injured a lot?"

A sudden silence washed through the atmosphere, and she could tell that they wanted to answer this delicately.

"Wolven heal quickly, shifting between both forms takes care of 90% of a wound. The other ten percent doesn't take long to heal. Yes, we do get injured, but it's insignificant. Sometimes there's a persistent injury. Take me for example. A beta once knocked me from under my feet and damaged my knee. It healed, but another one saw the weakness and aimed to injure me in the same place. We heal fast, but persistent and repetitive injuries are like human wounds, they ache and are always a sore area. The trick is to cover yourself during a fight to ensure that your weak spots are always protected. Sometimes easier said than done, but it's a necessity. Sometimes taking the defensive stance is better in the long run," Shane said.

"We'll always tell you the truth, Emma," Dante said huskily, his earnestness shining through, "even if it doesn't show us in a good light. We'll always be honest with you. Cementing our relationship on a bed of lies is not how mate pairings work. Regarding challenges, there's no real reason to worry. We're born as Alphas and Betas, Betas stay in that position because that's what they are. They're not as strong as Alphas, and, although it's a pain in the butt for us, it reassures the pack that their Alpha is still on the ball."

She smiled at them. "I know you won't lie to me. I appreciate your honesty, but I already know you're trustworthy. I don't doubt that. It's just the pheromone that concerns me. I know you say it's not even an issue, but *you* have to understand, I've made my life in the world of science. Rational, clinical, and practical as it is. It's unthinkable enough that you're Wolven. That I've seen the proof for myself is incredible. But soul mates?" She blew out a breath. "It's just taking me a while to compute."

Shane nodded and cupped her face in his hand. "You have all the time in the world."

She smiled at him then sighed. "I know. That's what is wonderful. I think I'm going to go for a nap. You guys are exhausting me!" Emma stood up, leaned over the table, and kissed Dante in gratitude for a lovely meal then left the table and departed for her room.

Quickly stripping off her clothes, Emma jumped into bed and settled herself within the goose down with a sigh.

* * * *

As soon as he touched her, she recognized Caden's

scent. It was indescribable, just as Shane's and Dante's were. Earthy and musky, it set her body alight. His touches only inflamed her. Rolling her hips into the bed, she moaned softly as his fingers parted her pussy lips and gently stroked her. Caden was a sensitive lover, every touch filled with love, every caress filled with emotion and a need to please her.

His lips brushed against hers, so softly it felt like butterflies wings fluttering against her cheek. Sighing luxuriously into the press of his mouth, she opened herself to him, gently touching the tip of her tongue to his and stroking it along the length of the muscle. A soft ripple of delight oscillated along her being, magnifying every sensation and slowly enhancing her desire.

It was the first time she'd ever felt as if she was being made love to. Oh they'd fucked her and at times had cherished her and now, she'd come to realize that she wasn't just a random quick lay for them. But this, this was so different. Even the past two nights spent in Dante's and Shane's arms didn't equate to this. They'd loved her, but not like this.   Treating her like a goddess, Caden's hand and mouth hesitant yet at the same time, sure as they touched her, wanting only to please her. It set her body aflame like nothing else had.

It was wonderful to luxuriate in his presence, his fingers tweaking her clit, rubbing it and clinching it between two fingers until she had to moan in wonder. The digits would slip down, down until they pressed inside her, touching the neck of her womb and scissoring pleasurably within the tight orifice. The wetness would transfer from her pussy to his fingers and his touch on her clit would be enhanced by the sheer sloppiness of the act. Maybe she should have felt uncomfortable by the copious juices that seemingly flowed freely from her body, but she didn't. Merely reveled in his effect upon her and she knew that he wasn't discomforted by it, that he too enjoyed the sign of her pleasure.

His mouth dotted tiny kisses along her jaw, down her collarbone, then licked singly at her nipples, reverting to the kisses as he trailed them down the length of her torso. His hands gripped her thighs and spread them slowly apart, tugging her slightly so that her hips could curve upwards and allow him to spread her further open.

The first touch of his tongue against the tunnel between her pussy lips made her shudder. It languidly rolled up and down, sometimes fluttering inside, sometimes pressing gently against her clit. Her breath hitched, and she alternated between panting and not breathing at all. It wasn't the first time they'd gone down on her, but it felt so different, so special. It was so amazing that small orgasms would sporadically erupt from inside her very depths, the irony being that she didn't actually realize she was climaxing. Those small orgasms were prized highly amongst human women, but Wolven were used to making their women explode with need, case in point with Caden. His mouth would work her into frenzy, touching everything and leaving nothing free from his tongue. He would then stop and she would cry out in frustration, thighs clenching tightly in warning around his head.

Never had she felt such abandon, so completely unselfconscious, and when he removed his mouth from her cunt and kissed her, she delighted in the touch of his wet face against her lower jaw. Perhaps she should have been revolted, but the sheer earthiness of the act was amazing. How could she be ashamed of something so fundamentally right. The answer was, she couldn't.

The clash of their mouths was faster this time, both of them ready and aching for Caden's possession, waiting for the thrust of his cock into her tight, tight pussy. On a frustrated groan, Emma's hand scooped down and grabbed his dick, pressing it against her clit and along the line of cunt, she drenched him in her juices, making the whole act slippery. They both shuddered at the sensations that echoed throughout them from this simple yet powerful touch. Her hand moved further down his cock, engulfing his balls within the palm of her hand was difficult but somehow she managed to roll the two together, pressing them together to create more friction.

He gave a deep groan and pulled away from her mouth to rest his head against her shoulder. "Fuck, mate," he shuddered, tilting his head to press a kiss to her neck.

She felt the nip that followed and her frame was suddenly racked with a small quiver.

That little sensation hurried the momentum along, suddenly she was spreading her legs further apart, pulling at the tendons in her groin as she rocked her hips hungrily. Her hand tightened and she grunted, "Caden, darling, please." The words were simple yet effective. When he lifted his head, dilated eyes stared back at her in the twilit evening and, within a few seconds, he'd impaled her on his cock.

He teased her unbearably by being so slow, thrusting to his own pace, ensuring that every inch of her felt the press of his hardness. It drove her fucking insane, she needed him to hammer into her. To fuck her. For his hips to ram himself deep, working himself further and deeper than ever before.

Her eyes must have transmitted her need, for suddenly his pace quickened, just a tad. But the speed incremented slowly until every thrust made her moan, every twist of his hips made her quiver. Alternating between a slow thrust and a fast plunge, she quickly saw stars behind her eyes. It was such an implosive feeling, it felt as though her body was going to stop working. She could now understand the phrase, *le petit mort,* because it truly felt like dying. As though her body could not take anymore, that it had to stop just to cope with the barrage of feeling.

Her pussy swallowed him, engulfing him in wet warm muscle. The soundtrack behind their love-making was shockingly indecent but wonderfully arousing. The act touched each of her five senses. The lick of her tongue against his salty skin. The pressure of his flesh against her own. The sight of his lean muscled body overpowering hers. The sounds of his thrusting into her wetness. The scent of the act intensely musky. They all combined into one powerful sensation, and it was intoxicating. Immediately she exploded around him, her cunt clenching and grabbing at his cock. Her breathy moans turning into loud shrieks of lusty release. Her arms clutching at him greedily. Her mouth gaping in sheer wonder at the power of this climax.

Head rolled back into the pillow, the final straw as was usually the case where these three men were concerned, was the feeling of their release. She imagined the white explosion filling her, running down her channel, mingling with her own juices and it just enhanced everything. Frowning in sheer disbelief, she gave a weak cry and fell back limply into the bedding.

Chapter Eight

Stretching sumptuously into the down-filled bed-linen, Emma cracked an eye open and squinted into the sunlight that was flooding through her bedroom windows. Turning her head to the side with a smile, she frowned as she discerned that she was alone in bed. She raised herself on to an elbow and looked around the room thoughtfully. Chuckling a little as she realized that she'd searched the room for his presence, she rolled her eyes a little self-consciously. They were truly driving her crazy!

It was strange to awaken alone. After all these years of resting in a solitary bed, she'd rapidly become accustomed to their presence, had even come to enjoy it and now felt secure with them lying beside her. These last few days had been so wonderful, waking in their arms, close to them throughout the night. Being held within their embrace while she slept. She sighed softly and felt disappointment flood her at her lone presence in the bedroom. Dropping back against the bed, she stared at the ceiling for a few moments, looking at nothing in particular as she pondered where he was. On another sigh, she grimaced as an unsavory thought entered her mind. One that she didn't want to even contemplate and, after all these days together, wasn't worthy of them. The insidious thoughts were: Had the pheromone finally worn off? Had they left her? Had her worst nightmare become a reality?

For the first time since she'd even contemplated creating a pheromone to help the wolf population of the world, she resented the damned chemical. Why had the stupid thing leaked on to her? If she could turn back time and stop the damned spray from emptying on to her hand, she would have done it! It would have been so wonderful had she known that their feelings, their intense lust for her was exactly that, for herself alone. Not because of some stupid chemical! Slamming her clenched fists against the bed, she closed her eyes tightly and tried to fight the thoughts that threatened to overwhelm her.

Quickly scrambling out of the bed, as though she was trying to run from her own thoughts, Emma raced out of the bedroom and looked into each room in search of them. When she spied them in the kitchen, she blew out a deep breath and rushed back to her bedroom to pull on a baggy shirt.

God, the relief that rushed through her upon seeing them told its own story. She couldn't live without them, it was as terrible as that. She grimaced a little. Why did she always believe the worst from them? She knew full well that she classed them as her soul mates, yet she refused to believe that she was theirs! By disbelieving them constantly, she diminished their feelings for her, belittled them and classed them as not as true as her own.

She hated herself for it, the little niggles of distrust crept through her mind, slyly touching her worries and dragging them out of all proportion. She knew that although her distrust sickened her, it would permeate her system for a long time. Knew it instinctively.

When you loved someone, you opened yourself up to being hurt. It was normal, the ones you loved had the power to crush you and that was why it showed the greatest trust to give someone your heart. It was all part and parcel of being in a relationship. She would just have to stop allowing that distrust to engulf her and would have to grow accustomed to these awful feelings. Until she knew for sure that the pheromone played no part in their feelings for her, she was stuck. She had no real clue how long the pheromone could endure, so the threat of their feelings for her being a chemical manifestation wouldn't be going away any time soon.

With a little sarcastic smirk, Emma realized that these insidious feelings of worry, fear of abandonment, devastation at the prospect of living without them, were exactly the reasons why she had always lived alone, why she had never tried to get involved with any man. She just couldn't deal with losing someone she cherished, so the prospect of losing all three of them was a complete nightmare to her. Just thinking about it made her feel slightly sick.

She returned to the kitchen slowly, feeling a little despondent and a lot concerned. Blowing out a breath, she entered the room and sat down quietly. She felt their eyes on her immediately, but they didn't speak. Silence reigned for a few moments as one of them lay a plate laden with slices of toast in front of her. She mumbled her thanks and picked up a slice of the bread to nibble at it.

Shane sat down beside her. She didn't see him entirely, just his legs entered her vision, but she recognized them as belonging to him.

His hand came up to clasp hers. "Emma, Caden didn't hurt you, did he? Sometimes our feelings for you can overpower us. I'm sure if he did that he didn't mean to."

"Shane! Of course I didn't hurt her. For fuck's sake!"

He ignored Caden and continued, "If he did, I promise to kick his ass."

That comment brought a smile to her face.

He chuckled. "See, that cheered you up a little."

Emma placed an elbow on the table and leaned on it. She continued to eat her breakfast although it tasted like ashes in her mouth. She sighed and kept her head bent over the table, her eyes averted. "Don't be silly, Shane, of course Caden didn't hurt me! He wouldn't even do it by accident, and, I think, if he ever did, he'd be kicking his own ass. He wouldn't need you to do it for him!"

"Glad to see that my mate realizes I would never hurt

her, even if my cousins fucking don't!"

"Shut up, Caden! If it's not him, then what's wrong?" Dante asked quietly.

"Nothing, there's nothing wrong. I'm just feeling a little weird, that's all." It didn't feel right telling them the truth, telling them that she feared losing them, that she loved them, that she didn't think she could live without them.

She knew they weren't pleased by her comment, that they would have preferred a more concrete answer so that they could go and slay whatever particular dragon was annoying her. But she wanted to keep her feelings to herself. She had been so up and down these last few days that she herself had no clue whereabouts she actually was! So she doubted that they would be able to understand either.

She sat silently and ate her toast, a halting conversation started up around her. One she was glad to stay out of and so, she grabbed her plate and stood up, hurriedly leaving the kitchen without a word and retreating to her lab. She ate the remainder of her breakfast in silence. She didn't particularly want it, but she needed some sustenance to keep her going over the next few hours.

It seemed incredible that considering how deeply she'd entrenched her life in wolves and their existence, that now, she had practically no time for her work. They had overtaken her mind and had prevented anything else from registering. To just sit down and concentrate on her experiments was becoming practically impossible. She just couldn't seem to focus on her work or the damned pheromone. It was as though the chemical had caused her so many fucking problems. Where Caden, Dante, and Shane were concerned, she wanted to just wipe it clean from her memory banks. No way could she even contemplate concentrating on her experiments. The day before it had been so hard to think about any of it, but she'd managed. Today her mind was filled with unpleasant thoughts. She just knew that she'd get zero done.

It should have annoyed her, the extent to which they had taken over her mind, but she accepted it as she accepted they were werewolves. It was just a fact of life, another one that she just had to become accustomed to. As independent as she'd once been, that concession was huge. It seemed incredible how her life had turned upside down and within such a short space of time. More incredible was the fact that deep down, she didn't really mind. Never had she believed herself to be so susceptible to falling in love with a man, never mind men!

With a glum look around her lab, she settled down on to her lab stool and put an elbow on the work surface. It seemed ridiculous to give them such precedence in her mind, but she had no choice. She couldn't remember another time in her life when she'd been so emotional, so hormonal. Pondering that thought for a moment, she tapped her fingers against the top of her work surface and frowned. It wasn't just the sex, because her emotions had started to overcome her during the second day. When they'd already slept together. If it had been, then surely during that first night she would have started to feel a little odd . . . .

Like Shane had said, it could be the mixture of her DNA with theirs, but she doubted it. Never having been in a such an intense sexual relationship before, taking precautions hadn't been a necessity. With a startled gasp, she realized that not one of them had taken precautions. None of them had used a condom. . . . Was she so hormonal and emotional because she was pregnant? That was a disconcerting notion.

But they were Wolven. Could they even impregnate her? Scowling at the thought, she wondered what the hell was going to happen now. Slamming a fist against the counter, she swore angrily. So many complications! This complication frightened her more than anything though, because now, if they left her, if she was pregnant, she'd have a baby to support and care for all by herself!

"Dammit all," she whispered tiredly and blew out a weary breath.

Despite her concern, a subtle desire crept its way through her and lodged itself deep in her heart. For was there anything more wonderful than becoming pregnant by a man she loved? On a sigh, she realized that whatever happened, if she was pregnant, she would consider herself lucky to have that gift for it meant that she would forever have a piece of them. Her child would always link them to her, and even though it was something else she would have to deal with, if she was pregnant, she wouldn't wish otherwise.

She dropped her head on to the work surface. How had everything become so damned difficult?

Too upset to work, Emma finally retreated to her bedroom. She would have relaxed in her living room, but they'd all been sitting there, deep in concentration. Each man had a bundle of papers on their laps, and they were intermittently studying them and talking. Having left the door open, she could hear them, and the guttural Russian dialect echoed throughout the cabin. It was so incredibly sexy that it pissed her off. They had no right to be so fucking sexy while she was facing one of the largest quandaries of her life!

No, they had settled down to work, had managed to actually get on with something productive. While she was over thinking, over complicating everything! She lay here contemplating the future and be she pregnant or not, her life was for forevermore tied up with theirs. It infuriated her that they'd managed to do something she hadn't been able to-concentrate! Lips pursed, she scowled at the ceiling and listened to them talk. Not understanding the language, she had no idea what they were discussing and didn't really care. She didn't think they were speaking in Russian to be rude or to hide anything from her, it seemed like the usual custom when they were together and she wasn't in the room.

Lunch was coming up, but she wasn't at all hungry.

She was way too damned upset to eat. How could she even contemplate food when her life was so fucking messed up? Rolling over on to her side, she stared out of the window and studied the light filtering through the trees. It was a beautiful view, one that had always relaxed her, but at this moment, nothing could relax her, nothing could calm her down. Such turbulence disturbed her, and, although she tried to nap in an effort to distance herself from her worries, she just couldn't find enough inner peace to fall asleep.

She tensed a little as she heard one of them walk down the hall and managed to relax before one of them popped their head around the door.

"Emma?"

It was Dante. She almost smiled. They'd sent the mediator.

"Yeah?" she answered quietly.

"What's wrong?"

Flinging herself over and on to her back, she sighed despondently. "Nothing, Dante."

"Emma, you're my mate. I not only have only to look at you to know that you're sad, but I can feel it too. I won't be satisfied until you tell me what the hell is going on. So, I let me repeat myself, what's wrong?"

"There's too much to talk about, and I really can't be bothered," she protested angrily, slamming her hands down against the linen. Then damning herself for answering him when she didn't really want to, she softly continued, "I'm scared, Dante."

He hesitated, but then moved to the side of the bed. "Why?"

She rolled back on to her side, away from him as he sat down on the side of the bed. "Why do you think?" Emma shivered a little as his hand settled on her thigh. No matter how angry she was at them, they could still set her alight with passion at mach speed!

"Emma, I can't help if you don't tell me what's wrong."

The hand that had rested against her side now began

a sweeping path along the curve of her waist. She felt him move, felt his naked torso press against her as he fitted himself to her. Her back to his front, her legs curved around his, his head resting on her shoulder. They couldn't have been any closer together, and a part of her sighed in relief, she always felt good when she was close to one or all three of them.

His new position meant a change of locale for his hand. Now, instead of resting on the innocent location of her waist, his hand came up to cup her breast, before swooping down over her midriff to play with the crotch of a pair of sleep shorts she'd shoved on earlier after quickly showering. His hand played with the waistband of her shorts, tugging at the elastic waist, letting it snap against her skin. His fingers tunneled underneath the material and her breathing became heavy from the promise of his touch, and soon it was impossibly intense in the otherwise silent room. His hand smoothed underneath her panties, trailing over the softness of her pubic bone to trickle down between her thighs.

His knee nudged between her closed legs and she gladly separated them, allowing him to keep them open by staking her down to the bed with that heavy thigh tucked between her own.

His fingers were gentle as they softly stroked her clit, teasing it enough to make her hips roll but never making her beg for his caress.

He seemed to understand where she wanted, no needed, him to touch. Never focusing too long on one spot, never touching her in the same way for too long either. Very soon shudders of longing oscillated through her and her hand clamped down on the one working between her thighs. "More," she whimpered and pressed back into him, groaning as she felt his hard cock brushing her back.

He worked his hand out from underneath her shorts and moved away from her back, shushing her as she tried to cling to him. Quickly he pulled the shorts from her legs, stripped her of her panties and then grinned. "I love that shirt on you, you wore one like it yesterday, didn't you?"

She smiled and nodded at him. It was another A-shirt, simpler in design this time and appropriate for bed. It clung to her like a second skin. Arching her back, she felt engulfed by pleasure as his eyes shone at her sensuously, obviously taking in the picture of her bare to the waist but covered tightly by a clinging shirt. His hand moved to cup her breast but then quickly slid down to her pussy. For a moment they seemed to concentrate there. Two, three, four fingers being plunged into her, filling her totally, the sensations exploded against her. Then he would thrust them inside her and a moan would escape her as a long slow trickle of her juices would trail between her butt cheeks. This continued for a few minutes until she felt so wet and so turned on that she had begun to moan feverishly on the bed.

Having spread her legs as wide as they could possibly open, she undulated on the covers, but he was focused on driving her insane. When his fingers moved away from her cunt and dropped down to play with her butt hole, she shivered as he worked all the juices into that one orifice. It turned her on immensely to know why he'd worked her so fiercely. All of a sudden, he growled something in that Russian language that made her pussy quiver with longing, and soon Caden and Shane were walking into the bedroom. Shane immediately headed towards her, his mouth clinging to hers before leaning down to bite at her cloth-covered nipples.

His hand joined Dante's, and she couldn't prevent the husky groan that vibrated against Shane's mouth as both men touched her simultaneously and in such intimate areas. Her eyes popped open as she realized that Caden wasn't taking part. Shane had taken possession of her mouth, so she had to angle her head to see what he was doing. Her eyes widened as she watched him jacking off. Fuck. Seeing him touch himself was the sexiest thing she had ever seen in her life. Tugging her mouth from Shane's, she demanded, "Enough! Fuck me," then less imperiously, she pleaded, "Please!"

Immediately they answered her demand, spinning her over so that she rested on her belly then lifting her so that Shane lay underneath. Feeling the hard press of his body against hers made her moan a little, she worked her chest against his and groaned again as the shirt deadened a lot of the sensation. Emma had no chance to complain, as Shane immediately plunged into her. Dropping her head on to his shoulder, her mouth worked silently. She rolled her hips to accept his presence, but the press of him against her swollen tissues seemed to double his size inside her. In what seemed a common act, she bit down hard on his pec and enjoyed the growl that vibrated through his chest. It inspired all sorts of possessive feelings and she delighted in it.

Shane didn't move, just lay there silently. Suddenly she realized why. Dante's hands were spreading her butt cheeks, she could feel his hands, wet from her juices, prodding her ass, lubricating her. Such an intimate process shouldn't have turned her on, but it did. God, it did. She had to close her eyes against it, had to work hard to keep still and allow him to continue preparing her. It was a groan of relief that escaped her mouth, when she felt the blunt head of his dick rest against her butt hole. She expected the tight squeeze, had known it was coming, but she couldn't help but groan gutturally at the large intrusion. It was one of those moments, where you wanted to escape. Had to escape because you felt as though you were being rendered into two. Both men's breathing was heavy but they didn't move, allowed her to accustom herself to their presence inside her. For some reason, today they felt inordinately larger than usual.

When she drooped against Shane's chest, she felt her

head being turned to the right and her mouth being conquered by Caden's. As the other men began to thrust, Shane filling her to bursting before pulling out and Dante's cock taking over his role; Caden took all her concentration. His mouth was quick, faster than usual, normally he was a tender kisser, every caress jam-packed with emotion. This time, it was a lusty kiss he pressed to her mouth. His lips working hers hungrily, their tongues dueling for supremacy. It was such an energetic session of love-making that a buzz of adrenaline coursed through her veins. Feeling them fuck her, their presence in her body's every single opening, made pleasure combine with adrenaline in a heady cocktail.

It didn't take long for them to work her up into such a state where she felt like sobbing. She had no time to settle before they'd begin thrusting heavily then changing pace, her mouth always occupied by Caden's. Their very possession of her used every single ounce of energy, they kept her in such a state that when a climax finally rushed through her, she accepted it and welcomed it with relief. Every muscle in her body was tense, every limb stiff and unyielding. She felt them cum, even felt the splash of Caden's seed against her side, but she didn't really notice it. Having retreated inside, where the release was working its magic, she basked in the sense of repletion.

* * * *

In what had become their usual sleeping position, Emma had awoken atop Shane. Her legs clasping his and her head resting on his pec. It should have been an uncomfortable position, but the sense of closeness took any discomfort away. She awoke to the realization that she'd never slept so well as when these three guys shared her bed. It could have been that they wore her out, or it could simply be that she felt so cosseted, so protected and dare she say, so loved that a good night's rest was easily on the cards.

She'd managed to disentangle herself from them and

had jumped from the bed without disturbing them. Looking into the leafy wood, the sunlight filtering through the tree canopies, she didn't know how she'd managed to leave the bed, then leave the cabin without having awoken them. Normally the slightest movement had them on edge, she must have really worn them out, she thought on a grin.

It was nice to be at peace again in the wood, she'd always loved it and the last time she'd been here, a rush of calm serenity hadn't overtaken her as it usually did. Maybe she was feeling more settled on the inside. She didn't know, but, either way, it was a relief to know that the wood still held a place in her heart.

Breathing in the fresh air was a heady pleasure. It was great to escape the confines of the cabin, she felt as though she'd been cooped up for far too long. She hadn't walked far, knowing that when they awoke and discovered her absence, they would quickly come and seek her out. No point in going too far to be dragged away ten or fifteen minutes later.

Planting herself on the leafy grass, she leaned back on her elbows and sighed at the new day. Closing her eyes to bathe in the sunlight, a smile graced her lips. She wasn't feeling so turbulent today, her emotions weren't as unsteady. In fact, she almost felt like her normal self, which was very gratifying. Being so jacked-up on her emotions wasn't normal for her. Normal was serene, not being overpowered by clashing desires!

Listening to the soft sounds of the woods, she wasn't aware of the man that was creeping up behind her until his hand came up to snatch at her mouth. As soon as the clammy paws touched her mouth, she recognized the scent as not being that of Caden, Shane, or Dante's. As ridiculous as it sounded, the pureness of their essence wasn't present here, and that realization sent a blast of fear charging through her.

The hands that gripped her tightly were rough. Immediately she pulled at them, tugging at them fiercely. He was shocked at the energy behind her fight, and she managed to pull his hands away for a second in which she screamed as loudly as she possibly could. It was cut short as this time, he practically punched her in the mouth to shut it and keep her quiet.

Feeling a little dazed, her body uncoordinated by the force behind his punch, he had the opportunity to grab her and drag her backwards. The jerking motion resonated through every bone in her body, the uneven movements combined with the dull ache at her jaw made her feel a little sick. Her stomach lurched, but it awoke her to the fact that he was hauling her away from the cabin, away from help.

Her lethargy now gone, she started to struggle, arms flailing, legs kicking out. She tried to bite at his mouth, managed to grasp some skin, but once more he moved his hand a little away and slammed it into her face. Her muffled cry spoke of her pain, and, deciding that struggling wasn't helping at all, she made herself go lax. The dead weight of her body made him stagger but didn't slow him down. It was at that moment that she realized he was Wolven.

His scent exploded in her nose, and it sickened her, literally made her bile rise in her throat. She could sense his lust for her, but not a sexual lust, an angry lust. A need for revenge. He wanted to hurt her in order to hurt someone else. The touch of his skin made her feel dirty, and she knew that the thought of hurting her turned him on. She could feel the press of his cock against her butt. Her stomach lurched once more at the thought of what possibly lay ahead of her. She could only pray to God that one of her mates would come and rescue her.

And they were her mates. She realized that now. They were her mates, and, more importantly, she knew that *she* was theirs. At this dramatic moment, she realized that, knew it in the very depths of her bones. It had taken something calamitous to make her realize that and for that she felt slightly ashamed.

In her mind, she shouted for them to come save her, told them that this man was trying to hurt her. She knew, just *knew* that they would come.

"This will show them, the bastards," the man muttered in her ear. He wasn't really talking to her, just mumbling to himself. "Teach the fuckers to mess with me."

He dragged her to a particularly dark area of the woods, the sheer lack of sunlight made it appear more sinister than it actually was.

It sent shudders of fear coursing down her spine.

He threw her to the floor.

Her arms instinctively came up to protect her head. She rolled to the ground with a grunt. She felt the landing jar through her entire system.

As she opened her mouth to yell out, he kicked her in the gut. Coughing hoarsely, she gripped her stomach but wasn't given much of a reprieve as he seemingly jumped to the ground and pounced. Hands grabbing at her clothes, he tore at her shirt and shorts, his strength really quite frightening as his hands ripped the tough materials away from her body. She tried to cling to the torn fragments of her clothes, but he persisted until she lay there in nothing but her bra and panties.

Her voice ragged, she gulped, "Why are you doing this? If-If it's about the pheromone . . . ."

"Don't be stupid, bitch. It's not about a fucking pheromone. It might get those fucking beasts hot, but a Wolven?" He sneered down at her semi-nude body. "No, the reason I'm doing this is because those bastards asleep in your cabin have fucked with my life. So why shouldn't I fuck with theirs?"

Her eyes wide, she realized that had she needed confirmation of why Caden, Shane, and Dante were in her life, she'd just had it. If she hadn't have just realized that they weren't with her for the chemical, then she knew now. The pheromone meant jack shit in the course of her love for them and theirs for her. It was a shame that it took being abducted and most likely raped for her to finally believe in them. She had to tell them that she loved them, needed them to know that. In the same way she'd yelled at them mentally to get their asses here, she hoped that they heard her love for them.

"I'm going to fuck you, and then I'm going to kill you," he said, smiling almost pleasantly at her. It freaked her out more than anything that had happened. The promise of death was in his eyes. It made the idea of just rape seem like a more gratifying option. What a joke!

His hands started to grope at her breasts. She thanked God for her bra at that moment, but her relief was short-lived as he clawed at that scrap of material. She cringed and then mentally screamed at herself to start acting defensively, her hands shooting out to punch him, slapping him wherever possible. She tried to knee him in the groin and managed to glance off his thigh, but he used that move to his advantage. Clutching the knee she'd lifted, he used it to spread her legs, and she damned herself for enabling to get in between her thighs. He practically dropped himself between her legs. The close proximity allowed her to claw at his back. Digging deep, she tried to gouge at his skin.

Imprisoning her hands in just one of his own, he jerked them upwards, dragging her torso from the ground and slamming her back down. Her head jolted awkwardly against the ground, and this time she saw stars. Dazed, she lay flaccidly on the forest floor and had to close her eyes against what was about to happen. His hand clamped down on her breast, twisted the nipple harshly. Her face scrunched up, and her eyes closed against the hideousness of what was happening to her. She refused to cry, although the tears wanted to well up and pour down her cheeks, she refused to show him her fear. It was bad enough that she kept reacting, trying to free herself from his hold.

It didn't matter how she tried to stop him. He kept on touching her, kept on groping her. His free hand had already clawed her panties away. His fingers touched her intimately, and, as she turned her head away from him in revulsion, she realized that both of his hands were occupied, and she let out a quick scream.

He reacted as ruthlessly as he had before. Lifting her from the ground by her wrists and letting her drop back down again, his hand went to clutch at her hair, and he slammed her head against the forest floor, stupefying her momentarily.

She blinked her eyes hard at the blur of figures that seemed to rush out of the trees and towards them. For a moment, she freaked out as her eyes cleared and she saw the three wolves converging upon them, growling and snarling as they raced toward them.

Screaming as one pounced, launching itself into the air to land jarringly against the man atop her, she quickly scrambled away, her feet fumbling to gain purchase against the leaf-strewn floor. She slammed herself against a tree trunk and cried out as the man transformed into a wolf and attacked Caden. She instinctively knew it was him who'd pounced on the guy, and she watched as they fought, biting and snarling at each other. Dante and Shane soon joined in, and she watched with a crazy mix of fear and wonder as all three effectively crushed their enemy.

A pervading sense of confusion worked through her mind. Why had she been attacked and by who? The questions wouldn't go away. Yet at the same time, she felt a little detached, feeling both safe yet fearing for their lives was a strange way to react to this deathly situation. She knew that they would protect her, could feel it instinctively. Knew that they'd rather die than for even one single hair on her head to be 'hurt'. She watched in awe as they sliced at him with claws and bit huge clumps of fur out of his hide.

Even though the man had tried to rape her and wanted to kill her, she shouted, "Caden! Dante!

Shane! Leave him!" Their heads spun around to look at her, mouths lolling slightly, even though their bodies were tensed and ready to attack. The lone wolf quickly took the reprieve and limped off. He looked in bad shape. She didn't know if he would survive or not, but she didn't want his death on her mates' conscience. Even though they would have probably have relished it.

Dante shifted first, the other two followed and ran over to her, he hissed, "Did he rape you?"

She shook her head fearfully, his apparent anger at her both shocking and concerning her.

"Where did he hurt you?" Shane asked angrily.

Her hands immediately rose to touch at what felt like her bruised and battered head. "He just kept . . . ," she hesitated. "I don't know, like he just kept slamming into my head or pushing it into the ground." She tenderly prodded at some sore areas and winced.

"Fuck," Caden said, grimacing as he removed her hands, "Baby," he hesitated then continued hoarsely, "are you alright?"

She nodded before bursting into tears and pushing herself into his arms. When they came up to engulf her, she shuddered and pressed herself into him. "He was going to kill me," she mumbled into his chest, "I thought I would never see you again. Who was he? Why did he attack me? I didn't even know him. Why did he want to hurt me?"

The tears she had tried so hard to withhold ran streaming down her face, sobs shuddered through her as, safe in her mate's arms, relief flooded her.

"Baby, that was never ever going to happen. He would never have gotten that far. That I promise you. His name is Kyle. He's a rogue wolf that tried to gain entry into our packs. He attacked you to avenge his eviction from our pack lands. It's a huge dishonor," he clarified as he whispered softly into her ear.

Holding her tightly, he nuzzled his face into her jaw, obviously seeking reassurance that she was eager to give. Slowly, he pushed her forwards, and, clinging together, with Dante and Shane two steps behind them acting as guards, they slowly made their way to her cabin.

"I love you, Caden. I had to tell you that." The words were mumbled against his skin, but he clearly heard it.

"Mate," he said, sighing deeply, *"I* love you, too. We all do.*"*

With a jolt, she absorbed his words, and, unable to help herself, she sobbed harder. "I thought you didn't," she murmured emotionally.

"Baby, we knew that," he said, his voice wry. "We're nearly there. Do you promise me you're okay? Do you need to see a healer?"

"I feel okay. I-I know what just happened was . . . ." She blew out a breath. "I'm fine. My head's sore, and I probably have a lot of bruises, but I'm so relieved to be with you again. I thought you wouldn't get there in time. I kept screaming for you and screaming for you. It was almost too late ...."

Awkwardly, Caden held her to him then bent down and lifted her legs so that he could carry her the remaining distance to the cabin. "I love you, mate," he breathed against her hair. "Never forget that."

Soon, he was walking her through her front door and took her through to the bedroom, laying her gently on the unkempt bed. With a gulp, she teased a little weakly, "You could have made the bed!"

Caden smiled a little then leaned down and reached for the blanket to cover her up. "Where's the first aid kit?"

"Kitchen."

"Dante! Bring the first aid from the kitchen!"

Dante brought the box in and handed it to Caden. Opening the box, removing some cotton balls and peroxide, he doused the cotton in the disinfectant. Lifting the blanket a little, he pressed the ball to the scratches on her legs. Hearing her hiss made him glare at her leg, then to Dante, he grunted, "I told you Kyle was dangerous, Dante. But did you fucking listen? No!"

Dante opened his mouth to respond, then looking at Emma, he lowered his head and breathed, "Yeah, Caden, you did. I didn't realize he would do this, though!"

"No," Caden conceded, "I know you didn't, but we should have handled him better at the time. The packs are at fault. They didn't accept him, we just had to enforce the decision. It didn't give him the right to do this though."

"What the fuck did he think he was doing?" Shane asked.

Emma answered hesitantly, "He said that he was fucking with your lives the way you'd fucked with his."

Each man closed his eyes for a second.

"Emma," Dante replied hoarsely, "Had I known you were in danger . . . . I can only apologize and beg for your forgiveness."

She reached out her hand for his, clinging to it, she whispered, "I know you didn't! Don't be silly. You can't be held to account for some crazy man!"

"No, but we should have protected you better, kept you safe. We know that rogues are out there, always a danger to any lone Wolven or their mate. That you got out of bed and left without waking us?" he shook his head despairingly.

"Dante! Stop it. All of you. I'm fine. It takes more than a few scratches to put me down! I-I promised myself that I'd tell you all that I loved you, each of you. Caden says you all love me and I, *I* know now you're my mates and that *I'm* yours." Squeezing his hand, she watched as Dante got to his knees beside the bed and pressed a kiss to her hand.

"Mate, you're my life, of course I love you," Dante rasped.

Shane leaned over to press a soft kiss to her forehead.

"And I love you, mate."

"I have to tell you something else, I only really realized just yesterday. But I-I think I'm pregnant . . . . I could be wrong."

"You are," Shane confirmed with a smile, "Second day."

"Second day?"

"You were pregnant by the second day," he clarified.

Shaking her head a little dazedly, she lay back against the bed and whispered. "I think I need a shower."

Caden finished up cleansing her scratches then stood up. Leaning over the bed he raised her into his arms and walked her straight into the shower. It all happened so quickly that Emma laughed. It seemed incredible that she could laugh so soon after what had just happened, but laugh she could. It was amazing how these men made her feel, how safe and protected. That would never change. Their coddling had made her feel better instantly.

"I take it you're showering with me?" she asked wryly.

"I don't want to leave you, and I want to clean that bastard from your skin." He lowered her to her feet then turned the faucet a little, wetting his hands only slightly. Grabbing the soap, he poured a little into the palms of his hands, rubbing them together, he created a lather and spread it over her breasts, arms, and belly. Then he dropped to his feet, dropped a little more soap on to his hands and cleansed her legs, tenderly he touched her intimately and cleaned her there too. Pressing his lips to her soapy belly, he whispered, "God, I don't know what I would have done if he'd . . . ."

Gently she put her hand in his hair and stroked the tousled locks. "Don't be silly. You don't have to think about it. I'm here and you're here."

He didn't reply, just shook his head a little before standing. Then releasing some more water out of the faucet, he washed the soap away, limb by limb. Focusing intently on her, he cleaned her completely. His firm strokes washed away the grime of the man, Kyle's touch, and the memory. In his arms, she almost felt as though the traumatic event had never happened.

After having showered, Caden carried her back to a freshly-made bed and tucked her in, before leaving her with a kiss on the cheek. Dante soon entered her room and curled himself around her before she fell asleep. During the night, another swap had been made. When she opened her eyes it was to discover that Shane now lay beside her. Hearing soft breaths, she popped her head over the side and laughed softly as she saw Caden on the floor and could only imagine that Dante was on the other side.

Looking at the three men, well the two that were visible she thought with a smile, she couldn't believe how bright the future looked. Their child in her belly, their love encompassing her, never had she felt so secure.

Yesterday had been an ordeal, that she wouldn't deny. She wouldn't even wish it on her worst enemy, but it had helped open her eyes to the truth. It shamed her that it took something so drastic to make her see something that was so clear, but it no longer mattered. Here she lay, in her little cabin, loved by these three powerful men, and she couldn't believe how truly lucky she was.

With a little sigh, she curled into Shane's side, her hand trailing down his torso to clasp his dick firmly.

Life was good.

THE END

Mandy loves hearing from her readers. You can email her at themandymonroe@yahoo.com

Other Available Titles by Mandy Monroe:
Dances with Wolves
In the Shadow of the Wolf
The Wolf Within

Read an excerpt from Dances with Wolves:

Dances with Wolves

By

Mandy Monroe

Chapter One

"No!" Jada yelled in frustration as the stench of burning toast filled her small kitchen. Rushing to the toaster, she popped the bread out and stared at the blackened bread with disgust. "Dammit!"

Flinching as the hot toast burnt her fingertips, she played handball with the two pieces and finally threw them down on the counter. Shaking her head, Jada scrunched her face in distaste as she scraped the black off her bread, but she hated waste and refused to throw her battered breakfast away. When she was done, she buttered it before taking a hesitant bite. Quickly brewing a cup of tea, she sipped at the drink to stop the indigestion from the butter she could feel licking its way around her chest before heading over to the small Juliet balcony that was the main feature of her apartment. The feature was the only thing that had sold her on the damned place. It was in the wrong area to be convenient for work. It was surrounded by married couples and families, and her friends all lived miles away from the place. But she'd loved the balcony on first sight, and, like the impulsive idiot she was, that had been that.

She leaned over the railing and sighed down at the sight of all the happy families enjoying the first day of their weekend. She wasn't jealous, not really, more resigned to the fact that she would never be a part of those happy trios and quartets she saw below in the gardens of her street. Closing her eyes, she took a deep breath, thrust the twinge of pain away and continued to drink her tea and people watch. She had never really fit in on this street and never would unless she had both a man and a baby backing her. To the married mothers, she wasn't an advantageous friend to have because she was both a threat and useless. She'd found out early on that they maintained the belief that every single woman was after their beloved husband, and she couldn't be useful enough to be called upon to baby sit in times of urgency.

It was a very isolated life she led in this building, one that reminded her of her infertility on what seemed like an hourly basis. But somehow, even though she'd had many an opportunity to move, she liked her apartment. She liked living here, despite the constant reminder of what troubled her most in life, which was why she'd stayed where she was for the past three years.

Maybe she was just a glutton for punishment?

Draining her cup of tea, she returned to the kitchen to

leave it in the sink and headed to her front door where she'd left the mail from the day before on the entry hall table. Sorting through the usual bills and junk, she quirked a brow in surprise at a thick envelope. She was quick to note that the stationary was very expensive and looked at the handwriting on the front of it. Smiling, she realized who the sender was. She glanced at the rest of the unimportant mail, discarded it on the table, and returned to her balcony to read the unusual letter.

Jada opened the letter slowly, excited. She never got mail unless it was a bill or junk. And this mail was special, she'd known from the handwriting that it was from her old friend Larissa. She read both the invitation and the cover letter. Shaking her head in exasperation, she couldn't help but smile as she read her friend's informal words which were in direct contrast with the formal, over the top invitation. Larissa lived in la-la land most of the time, cushioned by her father's wealth and love and now her husband's, but she was a lovely woman and a wonderful friend. It had saddened her greatly when Larissa had decided to leave America for good to marry and settle in the land of her ancestors, Scotland. That had been over two years ago and still she missed her.

With a grin, she scanned the invitation again. A thrill of excitement washed over her as she fingered the lush envelope.

I, Larissa Montgomery, cordially invite Jada Smith to a masquerade . . . .

There was something very child-like about Larissa, always playful and teasing. It was a quality that Jada had always enjoyed and now missed very much. Fortunately, getting hitched hadn't changed her friend one little bit. But she hadn't realized until this moment how large a gap Larissa had left in her life. Sure they still spoke on the phone and by email. Only last week they'd been instant messaging each other, but it just wasn't the same.

She reached for the phone hanging nearby on the wall of her kitchen and then perched her butt on the railing of the balcony and dialed her friend's number.

"Jada!" Larissa exclaimed, unable to conceal her excitement.

Jada couldn't help but smile as she replied, "Lari! I just got your invite. What's all this about? Why so formal?" she teased.

"Well, as you read already, it's a masquerade. That means I have to be formal!" she answered in exasperation at her friends questioning.

Evidently that was explanation enough. Jada shook her head at her friends reasoning. She'd figured out long ago that some things only made sense to Larissa. "Ah," she acquiesced, "but just how eccentric is this going to be? If I know you, which I do, you didn't tell me everything in your letter. What's really going to be happening at this masquerade you have planned?"

"I'm hurt," Larissa said, feigning indignation.

Jada was tempted to roll her eyes. She knew better than to think that she'd wounded Lari. It took a lot more than that to offend her friend.

"Not falling for it, huh?" she said a few moments later.

"Nope, come on, spill! I want all the details."

"You might be shocked if I tell you. I was sort of hoping you'd just come over and then find yourself unable to resist staying. Besides all that, you need a break, honey. You know you do."

"Oh God, what is it you've got planned now? Is there going to be some sordid group orgy or something?" Jada joked. As the silence down the line registered, she squeaked, "You didn't deny it! Are you really going to have an orgy? Larissa! What the hell? You'd better start talking."

"It's not an orgy, exactly. Don't forget, darling, I'm married and have a child. It's just a little get together for free time to play."

It was obvious to Jada that Lari was choosing her

words very carefully.

"We're all consenting adults, Jada, nothing illegal is going to go on. Besides, when was the last time you got laid?" Larissa asked bluntly before answering her own question, "I'll just bet I know when it was. I bet it was two years ago when you left David because you couldn't handle telling him that you can't have children. God, Jada, aren't you going insane? I know your body must be feeling the strain. I sure as hell couldn't wait two weeks for sex, never mind going two damned years without it!"

Jada heard a muted, 'Thank God for that,' in the background. She assumed Lari's new husband Alexander was listening in on his wife's conversation. With a groan, she mumbled, "Please tell me Alex didn't hear you say I haven't had sex for two years!"

"Darling, it's not like he didn't already know! Hang on a second." Then, in an aside, she said, "Alex, go away! Be thankful you get what you get and don't make fun of poor Jada."

Poor Jada heard Alex grumble in the background.

"Don't worry about Alexander, honey, he feels as bad for you as I do. Take it from someone who has a sex life, you need to come to this party just to cum!"

Larissa's laughter tinkled down the phone, making Jada want to grind her teeth. "And just what does Alex think about this orgy?"

"Well, I don't think he's overly perturbed about it, Jada darling, seeing as he's helping me organize the damned thing! We take part together. It's all about variety with some stability."

The last was said with such relish that Jada couldn't help but laugh at her friend's audacity. Shaking her head, she said, "This isn't the first one of these you've had, is it?"

Larissa hesitated before she spoke again. "I would have invited you before, but I knew you wouldn't come, so I didn't bother to embarrass you with having to refuse. This is either the sixth or seventh event we've had. We hold them as and when the need calls."

Jada frowned at the strange phrasing then sighed her acquiescence. "You're right. I do need to get laid. I reckon I'll be there."

Larissa smiled at the crankiness in her friend's voice and asked gently, "I know you were a size six the last time we met. Have you lost or gained any weight in that time?"

"Cheeky. I'm still a six. Why do you ask?"

"Don't worry about it, it's just your costume for the party. But don't ask me about it, I picked it out especially for you. It's a surprise that'll have to wait until you get here."

"Larissa," Jada warned, "you know I hate having stuff picked out for me. It's not risqué, is it? Dammit, why couldn't you let me pick out my own outfits?"

"Tut tut, I told you not to ask. I had to pick your outfits because I know you, you'd turn up in something that would make a nun look underdressed. Jada, just because you can't have a baby doesn't mean you have to dress like a schoolteacher. You're a sexy, beautiful young woman. None of that is diminished by your infertility. God, there's more usefulness to women than just as baby making machines! Getting back to what I was saying about the costumes, I've picked some appropriate outfits out for you. Some are old costumes of mine, so if you're not overly keen about them then you can swap them. But, don't worry, you know I'd never do anything to hurt you."

Jada smiled weakly. Larissa knew how to get down to the bone. "I know you wouldn't. Thank you. I'm grateful, I promise. You're sure this is a good idea though?"

"Of course it is! You'll have a fantastic time, and when you return to the U.S. you'll be feeling replete and sated, exactly how every woman should feel! Now, I have to go, darling, so take care and I'll see you when you get here. Have a safe flight." With that, Larissa quickly hung up.

Jada was left sitting halfway between the silence of her apartment and the noise of the families below. She got to her feet, feeling both weary and excited, an odd combination of feelings, but it was how she felt. She was excited at the prospect of something forbidden and yet strangely she felt tired when she recalled Larissa's words.

Her friend was right, she was young, could at times and when she tried, be sexy, yet she repressed the sensual woman because she couldn't let herself go with any of the men she dated. It went against all her principles to have casual sex. To her there was no point to love-making if there was no feeling behind the act. So because she didn't want to get involved in long-term relationships, because they only left her feeling heartbroken when they ended, she didn't involve herself in the short-term flings either. Perhaps this masquerade was just what she needed. She could enjoy sex for sex's sake, no need to place importance upon the feelings behind it. She just had to enjoy herself. But why did she feel like that was easier said than done?

She put the phone back in its receiver on the wall and headed over to her bedroom. She started to grab some clothes from her closet with the intention of packing her case immediately.

Perhaps the long dry spell wasn't so bad after all. It meant that she'd dedicated her free time to her work and therefore had a lot of vacation time saved up. She knew that Vic, her boss, would grumble, but would allow her to go. A lot of things had been getting her down at work recently. She'd been feeling the strain of having had no real vacation for the past two and a half years, and even Vic himself had suggested she take a break from the stress. Well, when she talked to him she would tell him that she was finally taking his advice and that she was off to bonny Scotland for a little while.

* * * *

With a deep inhalation, Jada allowed the fresh Scottish air to fill her lungs. Even in a congested train station the air was cleaner than the city she'd just left stateside! She looked forward to reaching Larissa's castle where the atmosphere was even purer and more rejuvenating.

She stood on the train platform, amidst the flurry of exiting passengers, and just relished being in Scotland again. It had been a long time, but it was lovely to be back. Shaking off the happy memories of times when her family had vacationed with Larissa's, she left the station and immediately saw a man holding a card with her name on it. Larissa had sent her an email saying that one of her drivers would pick her up because she had to greet other guests. She'd also casually mentioned a surprise for her again.

Jada walked over to the man holding the card and smiled. "I'm Jada Smith. Larissa Montgomery sent you, right?"

"Yes, Miss Smith. My name's McDougall. Welcome to Scotland, and, more importantly, welcome to the Highlands. Did you have a pleasant journey?" McDougall asked, his kindly face wrinkling as he smiled. "I hope you did."

"Thank you, M-McDougall, I did," she said his name hesitantly, unsure of whether it was his first or second name. Mentally shrugging it off, she answered his question, "My trip was as pleasant as can be expected, I suppose. It's a long flight and a long train ride, but I'm sure it will be worth it." She smiled at him and said conspiratorially, "Mrs. Montgomery said she had a surprise for me. Are you a part of that?"

McDougall chuckled and said, "Aye, if you'll follow me, miss." He led her over to a Victorian carriage and laughed heartily at her look of delight. "Mrs. Montgomery said you'd appreciate the finery of this old thing. Mr. Montgomery recently discovered it in one of the unused barns. He just had it renovated for use and the Mrs. said that you would enjoy making an entrance in it. May I be so bold as to ask whether she was right, miss?"

Jada grinned warmly. "Indeed she was, McDougall. Mrs. Montgomery knows me too well I'm afraid." She surveyed the coach and horses again with growing excitement. "Can I get in?"

"Of course, miss." He held out a hand for her to hold and helped her up to sit in the two-seated carriage. She couldn't hide the smile that shone from her face as the carriage rocked from side to side as the pair of horses shuffled impatiently. Although a terrible rider herself, she loved the animals. As McDougall climbed into the carriage beside her, he settled himself and said, "This is a curricle, miss. This particular one is around two hundred years old we reckon."

Jada peered out of the carriage and looked at it with fresh eyes. Two hundred years old! It was a two seater and wheeler, and the basic shape of the body was sledge-like, enough space for the passenger and driver and that was it. There was a canopy to protect the occupants from the weather, but little else. She didn't doubt that by the time she arrived at Larissa's, she would look like hell because of the wind whipping at her skin and hair, but it would be worth it, that she also didn't doubt!

As McDougall cracked the whip and the beautiful chestnut horses rocked in to movement, the curricle easily started on its way.

Settling back on to the seats, she was aware that the seats were padded comfortably and that the whole thing had to be more luxurious than the original. Having once read somewhere that the cushions had originally been padded with horse hair or straw, she knew immediately that the cushions she sat on were far too cozy for that.

Jada relaxed and enjoyed the roadside view, smiled when people pointed at them and the sight of a Victorian carriage on very modern roads. Soon she dozed off, jet lag catching up with her very promptly, and was just as quickly woken up by the rocking of the carriage. Coming awake with a jolt, she shouted over the wind, "Is everything okay, McDougall?"

"No need to worry, miss. It's just a rut in the road. We're nearly there. You should see the castle soon. Sorry to have woken you, but it was unavoidable."

She smiled her understanding and sat back against the seat once more to enjoy the view of the castle coming into sight. It was an awe-inspiring building. As a child, she'd been very jealous of Larissa, sure that living in a real castle meant that she was a real princess. Smiling at her childish folly, she began to reminisce a little. Their families had vacationed here often and their parents still went on holiday together, but as her father had allowed Larissa full run of the castle, they no longer met here. Now they traveled to other parts of Europe and far flung Asia. It was amazing really how long all of their friendships had lasted.

The castle didn't sprawl over acres and acres of land. It was very unusual in that it consisted of one tall building, five stories tall to be exact and attached to that was a smaller two story 'house'. The tall building was dotted with little windowed turrets, and small windows littered the walls, relics of the time when they were arrow-holes and crucial to the defense of the building. The castle had been built of a heavy cream stone that had weathered to a rosy and sometimes grayish hue, sporting a slated roof. Moss and lichen decorated the stone, and the 'house' had ivy crawling all over the front facade.

Just looking at the castle made her smile. Somehow the Montgomeries had managed to retain the old world charm of the place and install all the modern luxuries. Double glazed windows had replaced open air or lead windows, and she recalled that central heating had been added to heat the place and was used in conjunction with the huge open fires. It had been made into a home, and that made it all the more lovely.

As they drove over the driveway, expectation bubbled through her veins. She couldn't wait to see Larissa and Alex, and her little godson, Conall. It had been far too long since she'd seen them. Conall was almost three now. The last time they'd all seen each other had been at his baptism. It had been far too long.

She was annoyed with herself that she hadn't taken more vacation time to catch up with her friends. Even for Larissa's wedding at her castle home and Conall's baptism in London, Jada had only visited for the weekend and taken either the Friday or Monday off from work and then dragged herself into the office with horrid jet lag and had just gotten down to business.

Shaking her head in exasperation and annoyance at herself, she realized that she was more excited about seeing her friends than the party itself. Although she knew that she would enjoy herself, Larissa had stoutly told her that she intended to ensure Jada had sex at least twice. And once Larissa put you on one of her lists, that was it. So she had the prospect of some good sex ahead of her, but that didn't take her butterfly nerves away.

Maybe she was a prude now, either that or just dull. It had been so long since she'd been to one of Larissa's parties, to any party. Had she stopped remembering how to have fun? God, she hoped not. But the thought didn't ease her nerves. What did help was the knowledge that it was a masquerade. She couldn't make a fool of herself if no one knew who she was. In fact, that settled her stomach instantly. She was free to *not* be herself. She had the luxury of pretending to be anyone she wanted. To think so was dangerously thrilling, but she knew that that would enable her to enjoy the festivities to the max.

It was wonderful to be back at the castle, Jada admitted to herself as she jumped from the curricle as it pulled up outside the front entrance of the castle. For some reason it had always felt like a home away from home. Jada mentally reprimanded herself. She should have asked to come visit earlier than this because she immediately felt happier and more relaxed just being here. The last time she'd stayed at the castle was at Larissa's wedding reception, a time that had been both happy and sad for everyone.

It had been sad because Larissa had left America, her parents had left the castle for good, and moved permanently to another estate with a view to travel around all their properties that dotted about the globe, meaning that it was the end of an era.

It had been a happy because Larissa was so obviously in love with Alex that no one could wish anything but a long and lovely future for them both.

It was nice to be here knowing that she was just here to enjoy the festivities. Her emotions weren't tied directly into this event as they had been at the wedding or at the baptism.

"Jada!" someone shrieked so loudly that it actually echoed through the castle grounds.

Looking for the source and locating it, she reciprocated and yelled, "Larissa!" before running forward to reach her best friend. They collided laughingly, hugging, and crying all at the same time. "It's fantastic to see you again!"

"Tell me about it," Larissa said, grinning happily.

They stood looking at each other for a few seconds, feeling the bonds that tied them together as family and friends, and they embraced again.

"I just need to get my bag and then I can come join you," Jada said, smiling as Larissa grabbed her arm and linked them together.

Waving a nonchalant hand, Larissa stopped, turned around, and called out to the driver, "McDougall, would you please take Jada's bag to her room? Thank you so much." Turning back to Jada, she spoke eagerly, "I want to show you around, darling."

With that, Larissa dragged her forward through the huge wooden door.

Jada chuckled happily. "It's wonderful to be here. Why has this always felt like my second home?"

Pretending to think about it, Larissa tapped her chin and then said laughingly, "Hmm, maybe because it is? Oh, wait a minute. Here, you have to wear this, and I have to wear mine, as well." With a strong jerk, she tugged Jada into a small room at the beginning of the hall.

Jada peered around suspiciously but saw nothing in the gloomy room. She jumped when Larissa practically bounded onto her and dragged something over her face.

"Larissa? What the hell?" Jada asked, batting her hands like she would a pesky mosquito to push her friend away.

"It's a masquerade. You have to be masked!!"

"Why didn't you let me pick my own mask?"

"Look, I'm your fairy godmother during this vacation, and where your appearance is concerned, I definitely want to be in charge!"

She couldn't see that much of her friend in the gloom, but Jada was sure Larissa would be looking militant and her legs would be spread, hands on her hips. She couldn't help but smile at the mental image. When she wanted to, Larissa could be extremely domineering.

"For God's sake, Lari. I'm not totally helpless!"

Despite her words, both women could hear Jada's acceptance of Larissa's edict.

"Can we get out of here? It's way too dark!"

"Sure, come on. I still want to show you around."

On stepping outside the room, Jada blinked at the bright light and studied her friend's mask intently. It covered nearly all of her face. It was obviously supposed to be a butterfly, but it was like no butterfly she'd ever seen. There was nothing childish about the shape of the creature, totally unlike the usual B-shaped wings. These wings were made of wire metal, swirls decorated them, allowing peeks at the face underneath. Balls of the same metal littered the sweeping curling

edges of the swirls and bejeweled droplets fell from
the wings. She could see Larissa underneath, but at
the same time, it was easy to see where someone
wouldn't be able to recognize her. It was a lovely
mask and it suited Larissa's temperament and looks
perfectly. "What am I if you're a butterfly? A moth?"
Jada asked disparagingly. But she grinned at Larissa's
look of annoyance.

"I think you'll find that you look beautiful!"

"I'm sure!" she replied condescendingly.

Despite the beauty of the mask, Jada could see the
mega-watt glare and allowed herself to be dragged
away once more.

They walked down the hallway, which was swathed
with huge red velvet gold-edged banners. In a bizarre
way, they looked as though red wax had been dripped
over the walls. It looked magnificent, regal, and
exciting. The chandeliers above them sparkled
merrily. Candles were spread along the wall brackets,
adding a Gothic edge to the whole scene. The ancient
antiques that were littered about the place shone gently
in the candlelight. The castle was very obviously in
full party regalia.

As Larissa pointed out little changes she'd made since
having become *châtelaine* of the castle, Jada smiled at
the happiness that colored her every word. She was
glad that Larissa was enjoying her new life and home.
She had done wonders with her home. It had always
been beautiful, but with the added decorations it was
even more opulent and lovely.

The walk to her room shouldn't have taken long.
Whenever she'd stayed before, Larissa's family had
always given her the same room. She doubted that
custom would have changed, so she assumed that
Larissa was either taking her on a tour or she was
trying to force her to circulate. It was probably the
latter which was probably why it worked.

They passed several men and women along the way.
Some were short, some were tall, others were fat,

while still more were thin. There was obviously no
certain look for those in attendance. Until one
particular man passed them, she was very aware that
she'd found none of the men attractive behind their
masks.

Jada breathed a sigh of relief that this one man *did*
something for her. He was different than the other
men she'd seen, long and rangy with a leashed power
that was obvious in every move he made. Blacker than
black hair rippled over his skull, thick wavy locks
chopped short to control them. Tall with a
commanding presence, she felt her body quiver as their
gazes clashed. Golden eyes behind his mask shocked
her. Her mind argued that it was not possible to have
golden eyes. She must not have gotten a good look at
them. They had to have been an amber-brown color.
The only time she'd seen similar coloring was on a
documentary about wolves. Her lips quirked as she
realized that his mask was that of a wolf. She'd been
so stunned at the coloring of his eyes that she hadn't
really taken in the rest of the picture. Unable to resist,
she turned to watch him as he continued to walk down
the hallway, but he continued on his way and she
couldn't get a better look at him.

She summoned a mental image of the mask,
wondering even as she did if he would be wearing the
same mask the next time she encountered him. To her
surprise, she discovered her mind had very obligingly
recorded far more details than she'd realized.

Obviously, the mask was Japanese in design. Its
starkness was shocking. The mask lovingly followed
the contours of his face, leaving his lushly shaped
mouth and strong shaven jaw bare. It was wolf-shaped
in that the mask had a small snout that covered his
nose, the eye holes were almond shaped, two small
triangles adorned the very brim of the mask and acted
as the wolf's ears. It was white, stark and simple, yet
the designer had allowed for a thick line of red to
decorate the mask. It swirled over the curves of the

eyes, bracketed the snout. It looked shockingly like blood, as though the wolf had gone in for the kill, but she shook her head at that analogy. The mask and the man underneath were far too beautiful for that.

Their gazes locked once more as he turned to look back at her.

Jada shivered as pleasant darts of sensation rippled over her, pulsing through her pussy and peaking her nipples. She managed to detach herself from his gaze and felt like drooling over his predatory walk, each movement concise with a lethal edge to it. He looked dangerous. He looked sexy, and, God, she wanted him. Those darts of pleasure heated up as he managed to snare her gaze once more. She felt on edge, couldn't help but feel like prey he would love to devour. And, at the moment, she wanted nothing more than to be devoured. She groaned. It woke her from her trance, and she made herself ignore the man, turn, continue walking, and concentrate on what Larissa was saving. A shiver skated through her as the excitement began to wane.

"Are you cold, darling?" Larissa asked, a look of worry etched on her brow.

"Just a little. It's a lot warmer back home, you know?"

"I know." Giving a hearty sigh, Larissa gave her a pointed look then admitted, "It's one of the things I miss. Every other want can be eased. Food can be sent over, you'll visit when you can, and we talk all the time, but the weather!" she said, groaning loudly. "God, I miss the sun sometimes. It always seems to be gray, and when I think I can't stand it one moment longer, the sun shines and lights every dark corner and seems to make everything sparkle. The grass looks greener, the sky bluer, and, straight away, I'm happy again."

"I'm glad to hear it," Jada said, squeezing her friend's arm. "You deserve to be happy, honey. I'm glad you found Alex and that you love each other and now you have Conall! I couldn't wish for anything more for you."

"I know, Jada, that's why you're such a wonderful friend. I just wish the same for you. You're thirty, for heaven's sake, yet you act like an elderly spinster. I refuse to let you waste any more of your life, Jada, because that's what you've been doing. I won't stand for it anymore. I can't bear to think of you back in the States, working every hour on the hour only to come home to an empty apartment. It's just not right, and, moreover, it can't be healthy for you. You have to stop feeling inadequate for the rest of your life. You're so much more than a womb, darling. Look at you! You're beautiful!" Larissa forcibly grabbed her by the shoulders and shoved her in front of a mirror along the hall. "You've seen some of the guests. Not everyone can pull off a mask, yet, look at you, you're beautiful with or without it." She quickly pulled the mask away so Jada could see her before and after image.

"Larissa, I hear what you're saying. It's just a lot easier to say than to put into practice. How can I help but feel the way I do? Men have made me feel this way! I've been serious with three men since college, two of them ended it because of my infertility, and I ended the last before he could, because I just couldn't bear to tell him, I couldn't bear for him to know and then break up with me just like the others did. For me, splitting up is as inevitable as night turning into day. I won't deny that I want to have a partner. I just haven't found the right one yet one who accepts that I can't have kids, and, as you say, darling, I'm only thirty. There's plenty of time to find the perfect guy." Jada gave her friend a smile and then jokingly said, "By the way, I like the mask."

"And so you should, it's lovely!"

It really was lovely. The part that covered her face was very simple, like the eye mask she wore to sleep but with holes for sight. The edges were sharp and angular, a simple black satin. Gathered at the side of her head was a large cluster of black, green, and sable colored feathers contained by a pin on which lay a sapphire-colored gem. A long length of black satin ribbon fell from the sapphire pin. The feathers lay along the side of her face in a semi-circular pattern. There was something very art deco and 1920's about it, yet at the same time it reminded her of a Native American headdress.

She smiled before turning to her friend and kissing her on the cheek. "Thank you for caring, Larissa, and thank you for inviting me. I have to admit I was skeptical of your plans at first, and, although that feeling will probably return later on, at the moment, I'm looking forward to the masquerade!"

Made in the USA
Lexington, KY
24 October 2010